MEET THE FORTUNES!

Fortune of the Month: Brodie Fortune Hayes

Age: 33

Vital statistics: Six feet of maddeningly adorable British charm. He tastes of champagne and mint and...challenge.

Claim to Fame: The mastermind of Hayes Consulting, Brodie can make business troubles disappear. He is also known for stealing hearts.

Romantic prospects: "Brodie the Brit" has no interest in getting serious. Work is his mistress, the ladylove of his life.

"Alden Moore hired me to fix his Cowboy Country theme park. What he neglected to mention was that he put his daughter in charge of the project. I cannot work with Caitlyn Moore! I suppose her daddy had no way of knowing what, ahem, previously transpired between us. Success in business depends on keeping a clear head and a closed heart. And Caitlyn is simply too warm, too sensitive and too...much. Between her and all my newfound Fortune relatives, I am being bombarded by good intentions. How is a man supposed to get any work done?"

THE FORTUNES OF TEXAS: COWBOY COUNTRY—
Lassoing hearts from across the pond!

Dear Reader,

I live in central Florida with some of the nation's most established theme parks right in my backyard. I've seen how this area has grown and changed in the shadow of the mouse (and company). When I had the chance to write a Fortunes of Texas book that featured a cowboy-themed amusement park, naturally I was thrilled.

Too bad the good folks of Horseback Hollow are less than enthusiastic about Cowboy Country moving into town. What makes it even more challenging is when they discover one of their own, Brodie Fortune Hayes, is not only working to ensure that the park opens successfully, but that he could be falling in love with the owner's daughter, Caitlyn Moore. What's not to love? Caitlyn has a big heart and seems to understand the Fortune clan better than Brodie does. Still, it's a wild ride as the two work together to win the trust of the town—and each other.

I hope you love Caitlyn and Brodie's story as much as I enjoyed writing it. Please let me know what you think. You can connect with me through my website, nancyrobardsthompson.com; Twitter, @NRTWrites; and Facebook, facebook.com/nancyrobardsthompsonbooks.

Xoxo,

Nancy Robards Thompson

My Fair Fortune

Nancy Robards Thompson

HARLEQUIN® SPECIAL EDITION®

Special thanks and acknowledgment to Nancy Robards Thompson
for her contribution to the
Fortunes of Texas: Cowboy Country continuity.

ISBN-13: 978-0-373-65884-8

Recycling programs
for this product may
not exist in your area.

My Fair Fortune

Copyright © 2015 by Harlequin Books S.A.

Printed in U.S.A.

www.Harlequin.com

National bestselling author **Nancy Robards Thompson** holds a degree in journalism. She worked as a newspaper reporter until she realized reporting "just the facts" bored her silly. Much more content to report to her muse, Nancy loves writing women's fiction and romance full-time. Critics have deemed her work "funny, smart and observant." She resides in Florida with her husband and daughter. You can reach her at nancyrobardsthompson.com and facebook.com/nancyrobardsthompsonbooks.

Visit the Author Profile page at Harlequin.com for more titles.

This book is dedicated to all the Fortune fans
and to Susan and Marcia for making it happen.

Chapter One

February

"Brides or grooms?" the tall, handsome guy asked.

He had a British accent.

Caitlyn Moore had locked eyes with the tall hunk of gorgeousness only a moment before he'd moved across the room to stand next to her. The accent was the icing on top of an already delicious-looking bit of eye candy.

Too bad eye candy wasn't on her diet.

"I beg your pardon?" she said.

"Are you here in support of a friend or relative of one of the brides or one of the grooms? Or, perhaps, you're acquainted with all of them?"

When he'd said *all of them*, he wasn't kidding. There were four of each—this *was* the soon-to-be-famous

Grand Fortune wedding—and Caitlyn didn't know a single one of them personally. From what she'd heard, the Fortunes always did everything in a big way.

"None of the above," she said.

"So you're a wedding crasher, then?" Twin dimples winked at her when he smiled.

"No, of course not."

Dressed in an expensive-looking dark suit and crisp white shirt, the Brit had a cocksure James Bond air about him. He probably didn't have to work very hard at getting women to engage. Still, Caitlyn didn't feel like explaining that she hated weddings and wouldn't be here unless it was absolutely necessary. She'd come in place of her parents, who had received the invitation to Horseback Hollow's social event of the decade…in a town this small, it might even be the wedding of the century.

Tonight not one, but four Fortunes had gotten married on their parents' sprawling ranch. They'd exchanged vows on a huge outdoor stage that had been constructed for the ceremony. She'd overheard someone talking about how the large red barn on the property had been renovated especially for tonight's reception. The place looked like a magical wonderland lit by thousands of candles and twinkle lights. There were so many flowers she shuddered to think of the bottom line on the florist's bill. It might even surpass the catering bill for the sumptuous-looking buffet dinner, which she was going to miss because her objective was to sign the guest book and leave. No one would miss her if she left a little early, especially since she was there on a mission that might best be described as *keep your friends close, but keep your enemies closer.*

In this case, the Fortunes—all fifty jillion of them—were the enemy.

It still baffled her that the Fortunes, who had gone to such lengths to get the locals all riled up, making everyone believe that her family's venture, Cowboy Country USA, a Western-themed amusement park, was the root of all evil and would be the demise of Horseback Hollow, would invite her family to the wedding.

Her parents had regretted missing out, but her father had fallen ill this morning, and her mother had stayed home to care for him. Caitlyn had come to the wedding on their behalf, to represent the Moore family and Cowboy Country. She wasn't here to glad-hand and win people over, of course. She'd simply signed the guest book *Alden Moore and family*, a subtle reminder that Moore Entertainment was not the enemy. On the contrary. They wanted to be the good neighbor, getting along with the residents of Horseback Hollow, every one of whom, it seemed, had been invited to the wedding.

She looked at the Brit, who wasn't acting shy about eyeing her.

And that part of the saying that talked about keeping your friends close? Yeah. It definitely applied to this new friend.

A moment ago, she was sure her work here was done, and all she needed to do was wait for the brides and grooms to finish their first dance before she made a discreet exit; except now the hot guy with the cool accent was smiling at her like he found her utterly fascinating.

"All right, then, love," he purred. "What is your story?"

He pinned her with the most spectacular pair of blue eyes she'd ever seen before arching his right brow a fraction of an inch in a manner that suggested he was waiting for her to elaborate. And then there was that accent. Why had she always been a sucker for an accent? It was her libido's Achilles' heel.

"What?" she said. "Are you the bouncer here to throw me out?"

He crossed his arms and appraised her in a less than subtle way that had her insides going all warm and melty. She needed to stop *that* right now. Mirroring his stance, she crossed her arms and tilted her chin up, hoping for some self-preservation, but her warm and melty insides offered no structure. Her resolve started to slowly crumble under the heat.

"If you must know," she said. "I'm here by proxy."

"I didn't realize wedding invitations were transferable," he said. "Don't worry, I won't land you in it, because   " he leaned in and whispered in her ear "—really, I don't belong here, either."

I won't land you in it. He was so maddeningly, adorably British it was almost too much, and he was standing so close that she could smell his cologne—something that was probably expensive. Something vaguely green and woodsy—maybe sandalwood…and some cedar—and oh, so manly and delicious.

"So *you're* the one who doesn't belong here?" she countered. "How do you know I'm not the wedding police, ready to bounce *you*?"

His eyes glistened as his gaze made an even bolder

perusal of her body, meandering down the length of her and back up again. Her heart beat with the pulse of the music, and she reveled in this irresistible, magnetic physical awareness.

"Not in that dress, love."

His breath held a faint hint of peppermint.

"What's wrong with my dress?"

"Not a bloody thing."

He flashed a smile that showcased perfect white teeth, and there were those dimples again.

Oh, God, just take me now.

A thrill the likes of which Caitlyn had never experienced skittered down her spine, waking up places that had been sleeping for far too long. This was…fun. A lot more fun than she'd dreamed she'd have tonight.

As a waiter passed by with a tray of champagne, he grabbed two flutes and handed one to her.

"Thank you." She raised her glass to him, and he followed suit, clinking his to hers before they sipped.

She'd purchased the red dress and strappy heels on the fly this morning. Since she'd only planned on visiting her parents for a few days, she'd packed light and casual. She hadn't brought along anything that was appropriate for an elaborate Valentine's Day wedding. She'd been pleasantly surprised to find the flirty little dress in a boutique in Lubbock. With his eyes on her, it felt a whole lot sexier than it had when she'd tried it on and decided it would do. She hadn't really been excited about the dress or the thought of attending the wedding of four couples she didn't know. It had barely been a year since she'd called off her own engagement.

The only reason she'd agreed to come tonight was because it had seemed so important to her father. He'd asked her to represent the family because he thought it would be a sign of solidarity for the good folks of Horseback Hollow, or possibly considered a slight if no one from the Moore family bothered to attend. As if anyone would even notice in such a crowd.

Who knew she'd meet someone so fun to play with. Maybe she wasn't in quite as big a hurry to leave after all. Then again, if she knew what was good for her, she'd leave right now before she gave this Brit a chance to charm her new red dress right off her.

"What's your name?" he asked.

"Cait—" She always went by Caitlyn, but tonight it felt more fun to simply be Cait.

"Ah, as in *Kiss Me, Kate*?"

"Oh, are you a fan of musical theater?"

"Not particularly. I simply wanted to say that." Their gazes locked. "Kiss me…Cait."

For the life of her, she didn't know what came over her, because the next thing she knew, she was leaning in and claiming his lips.

She didn't even know his name, but she adored the taste of him—champagne and mint…and something else she couldn't name, something that made her lose herself a little bit and lean in a little closer. His kiss sang through her veins, sent spirals of longing coursing through her, causing the fire deep in her most personal places to rage.

It had been a long time since she'd kissed a man. Since Eric— No, she wouldn't think about him. Eric would not ruin this moment…or this night, which was becoming better and better with each passing second.

The sound of the bandleader inviting the wedding guests to join the happy couples on the dance floor edged out the interloping thoughts of her ex. When she pulled back, the reality of what she'd just done washed away any lingering residue of Eric.

She'd kissed a man she'd known for less than ten minutes.

And she wanted to kiss him again.

Bloody hell.

Those were the only words echoing in Brodie Fortune Hayes's mind as he locked lips with *Cait*. And he meant those words in the best, most reverent way possible. Just when he thought he'd seen everything, life threw him a curvy surprise wrapped in a sexy red dress. He was obviously finding it difficult to express exactly how much he liked this shapely little package. All he knew was what had started out as a night of familial obligation was turning out to be rather mind-blowing.

Cait pulled back just enough to gaze up at him through thick, dark lashes. She had the loveliest green eyes he'd ever seen. "By the way, what's *your* name?"

"Brodie," he heard himself murmur.

"Brodie the Brit," she said. "Nice to meet you. I'm Cait from Chicago. I'd shake your hand, but…" She leaned in and dusted his lips with a featherlight kiss.

Then she smiled up at him, looking rather pleased with herself.

"Charming to meet you, Cait from Chicago."

The band shifted from an up-tempo tune into a slow, sultry number just as he decided to lean in for another taste of those lips, but Cait pulled away.

"Listen," she said. "This has been fun, but I really should go now."

"What? But we just got here. Well, we just got *here*."

He reached out and ran the pad of his thumb over her bottom lip. "I'm quite eager to see where we'll go next."

She opened her mouth as if she were about to say something, hesitated then pressed her lips together, drawing her bottom lip between her teeth in a way that nearly drove him mad.

"Dance with me?" he said.

Of course, he wouldn't force her to do anything she didn't want to do, but he'd try his best to convince her.

"Just one dance," he said. "If you want to go after that, I won't argue."

He took her hand, fully prepared to let go if she protested. But she didn't.

As he led her onto the dance floor, he noticed his brother Oliver dancing with Shannon Singleton, the pretty brunette they'd sat with during the ceremony. Oliver seemed to be lost in the moment as he gazed into Shannon's eyes. But when Cait sank into Brodie's arms and he pulled her closer, his body responded, and then it was as if they were the only two people in the entire world.

They swayed to the strains of "Unforgettable" and

kept dancing close through a couple of fast songs, until the band decided to mix things up with a country-rock medley, and an overzealous guest, who was dancing with a beer in his hand, tried to demonstrate his John Travolta moves and upended it on the dance floor.

"Okay, what do you say we take a break?" Brodie suggested. "How about if I get us something to drink?"

"Actually, I could use some fresh air," Cait said. "It's a little stuffy in here."

With the number of people dancing and drinking in the confines of the renovated barn, it was a bit close. It was unseasonably warm for February. In fact, he'd heard his mum and aunt Jeanne Marie say it was as if spring had graced them with an early visit, which was undoubtedly fortuitous for the four couples who had said their vows.

"That sounds like a great idea," he said. "Wait right here. I'll get us some refreshments to go."

He tipped the bartender fifty dollars and was rewarded with a chilled, unopened bottle of champagne and two flutes. On his way back to Cait, he plucked a long-stemmed red rose out of one of the many free-standing floral arrangements.

He took the bounty back to where he'd left her, but she wasn't there. As he made a three-hundred-sixty-degree turn, it dawned on him that it probably hadn't been a brilliant move to leave her alone. He hadn't been gone that long, but if she really had wanted to leave, this would've presented the perfect opportunity for her to make her getaway. His gut tightened at the thought, but then he sobered. Really, if she had decided to go, it was for the best. He was set to return to London in two days. True, Cait of the magical lips had an unnerving ability to knock him void of all common sense, but really, what would they do two days from now when he boarded the plane to go home? The likelihood of him traveling to Chicago anytime soon was slim. Business was booming at his company, Hayes Consulting, the management consulting firm for which he'd sacrificed everything. It had been a struggle even to find time to come for the wedding. If truth be told, he wasn't happy about taking time off for four cousins he barely knew. It had only been a couple of years since his mother had discovered that she was adopted and had three siblings who had so many grown children that it seemed to be necessary to marry them off in bulk. Still, it had been important to his mother that he attend this affair. She was the one woman in the world for whom he'd drop everything. Plus, it was a chance to catch up with his brother Oliver.

All the negativity drained away when he turned and saw Cait with her wrap and handbag, making her way toward him in the crowd. She was still here, and suddenly nothing else mattered.

He handed her the rose.

"This is beautiful," she said, bringing the flower to her nose. "How romantic, sir."

Her eyes glinted and at that moment, Brodie was sure she was the most beautiful woman he'd ever had the privilege to set eyes on.

"And what else do you have there?"

"A spot of champagne. What do you say we get out of here? There's something I'd like to show you."

He started to offer her his arm, but his hands were full with the two glasses and the bottle.

"I'm intrigued." She laughed. "May I carry something?"

"I've got this." He set down the bottle and tucked each of the champagne flutes into his suit coat pockets.

"Let's try that again." He offered her his arm.

She accepted, and he led her out of the noisy reception.

Once they were outside, it was quiet, except for the faint sound of the party going on in the barn behind them. A few people milled about. A line of golf carts, which were there to drive the guests back to their vehicles after the festivities ended, waited at the ready several feet in front of the barn. The cart attendants sat at tables, playing cards as they waited.

Brodie and Caitlyn walked from the barn toward the pond on the east side of the property. The night was unseasonably warm for February, but despite the mid-fifty-degree temperatures, he thought he felt Cait shiver. She'd put her coat on over that fabulous red dress.

Still, priding himself on being a gentleman, he said, "Is it too cold out here? We can go back inside…or I'm happy to give you my jacket. You could drape it about your shoulders."

She shook her head. "Thanks, but no. Actually, the cool air feels great after being inside. With everyone dancing and all that romantic energy in there, it was a little bit warm. Besides, I wouldn't want to take a chance on breaking one of those glasses that you worked so hard to steal for us."

"I didn't steal them. The bartender graciously gifted them to us. He thought we looked like such a lovely couple."

"Oh, really?"

"That's what he said." Brodie winked and took a great deal of pleasure watching the color spike in her ivory cheeks.

"So you're an honest guy?" she said. "Does that mean I can trust you to lead me out into the darkness? You're not some deranged serial killer, are you?"

Brodie stopped, unsure for a moment if she was serious. "Well…no. Of course not."

But really, could he blame her? They didn't know each other.

She assessed him for what felt like an eternity.

"Where are we going?" she asked. "What is it that you wanted to show me?"

"There's a meteor shower tonight. Out here, away from the city lights, the waning crescent moon coupled with the clear sky provides excellent viewing conditions."

Her brows knit together, and she cocked her head to the side as if she didn't understand.

"A meteor shower," he repeated. "You know, shooting stars? I thought it would be…romantic." He rocked back on his heels.

"I know what a meteor shower is." She smiled. "What I didn't realize was that you're an astronomy nerd."

The light from the tiki torches that lined the path caught the teasing sparkle in her green eyes, turning them an alluring shade of jade, and it took everything Brodie had to keep from leaning in and kissing her again.

"I've been accused of being a lot of things in my life, but I must say tonight is the first time anyone has called me a nerd…or a serial killer. However, if you like nerds, that's exactly what I'll be tonight. Just for you."

"Just for me? What about serial killer?"

He narrowed his eyes. "Sorry, that's not in my repertoire."

"Good to know," she said. "Call me crazy, but for some reason, I believe you."

Suddenly, she looked away and pointed toward the sky. "I think I just saw one. Was that a meteor?"

"Indeed."

"What are we waiting for?" she said. "Let's go where we can see better."

She grabbed his hand, and he led her toward the open field by the pond.

When they stopped, they turned their attention up to the sky.

"This is a rather slow shower," he said. "There may only be four or five meteors per hour."

"What should we do to entertain ourselves in the meantime?" Her voice was low and raspy. There was something in her tone that made him want to suggest all kinds of inappropriate things. She seemed to read his thoughts because she reached out and ran her thumb over his bottom lip. He was still holding the champagne bottle and the glasses when she leaned in and brushed a kiss over his lips.

"If you want to do something like this," she said, "I wouldn't object."

Before he could stop himself, he caught her bottom lip between his teeth and teased it with his tongue.

"How about something like that?" he asked, his mouth a breath away from hers.

"That? Oh, yes, definitely *that*. And more, I hope. But first I'll need a glass of champagne."

He spread his jacket on the ground, and they sat down on it. He popped the cork and poured them each a glass of bubbly. They clinked glasses and settled into the silence of the first sip. He reached out and brushed a strand of long, dark hair off her shoulder.

She inhaled a quick breath and seemed suddenly shy. Even though he was dying to kiss her again…and again and again, he knew he'd be smart to slow things down until he was sure she was comfortable.

He gazed up at the sky for a moment, searching, until he found what he was looking for.

"See those three stars in a row that are close together?"

He leaned in so that she could follow where he was pointing.

She didn't pull away.

"That's Orion's belt. Do you know the legend of Orion and Merope?"

She shook her head.

"Orion, the great hunter, fell in love with Merope. He made a business deal with her father. In exchange for clearing the land of all the savage beasts, Orion would have Merope's hand in marriage, but Merope's dad reneged and wouldn't let Orion marry his daughter."

"Poor Orion," she said.

"Yes, the poor guy was stricken with such sadness. He couldn't get the girl off his mind. He wasn't watching where he was going and stepped on a scorpion and died."

She slanted him a dubious glance. "It that really how the story goes? I thought there was more to it."

"I thought you didn't know the story," he said.

"I wanted to hear your version," she said, leaning into him. "I was hoping you'd make it a love story."

"Oh, it is." He clamped his mouth shut before he could add something stupid like *this is a real-life love story, sweetheart. Love hurts.*

Instead, he continued. "The gods took pity, and they immortalized him and his dogs up in the sky as constellations."

He outlined the stars with his finger.

"They put all of the animals he hunted up there near him—like the rabbit and the bull. But they put the scorpion all the way on the opposite side of the sky so Orion would never be hurt again."

"What about Merope? What happened to her?"

"She's still there. She's a star that rides the shoulders of the bull. So he can always see her."

"You have a romantic heart," she said.

"Funny, others have claimed I don't have a heart."

"Well, they were mistaken, my romantic astronomy nerd."

She rested her head on his shoulder. Her hair smelled so good he breathed in trying to identify the fragrance… it was something floral…and sweet. The combination was intoxicating. He thought he could live happily here.

Just the two of them sitting close, sipping champagne under the inky starlit sky.

He slid his arm around her shoulder, ran his hand down the length of her arm. She tilted her head up and leaned in closer, tempting him. His lips found hers, and this time the kiss wasn't quite so gentle. She responded, her body pressing against his. The way they fit together might have brought to mind tired clichés like puzzle pieces or bugs in a rug, but he was too caught up in *her* to give it much thought.

All he could focus on was the feel of her…the taste of her…the all-consuming thought of what it would be like to make love to her…their bodies even closer than they were right now. Him buried deep inside her. Them moving to their own private rhythm.

He heard a sound—a low, guttural rumble—and realized he was the one making the noise. As if the force was driving him, he deepened the kiss. He couldn't get enough of her. She tasted like the champagne they'd shared. But there was something else… something uniquely her. And it was threatening to drive him crazy.

His hands slid from her hair down her shoulders, and he closed his arms around her, pulling her closer. He memorized the feel of her as he lowered her back, onto the ground.

"Are you okay?" he asked in a brief moment of clarity. He would never force her to do anything that made her uncomfortable. "Is this…okay?"

"I've never been better." She smiled up at him. "I

have a feeling I'm going to be even better very soon. So please don't stop now."

He held her gaze for a moment, until little pinpricks of longing injected him with a need so powerful it had him seeing stars. When he reclaimed her lips, it lifted him off the ground and into the heavens of lusty bliss. When was the last time he'd wanted a woman so badly that it bordered on greed?

On need…

He unbuttoned her coat and slipped his hands inside, savoring every inch of her—her tiny waist, her sexy hips. That red dress was all that stood between him and that glorious body. He slid his hands back up her torso, around her rib cage and paused underneath her breasts, giving her one more chance to slow things down, if she wanted.

God, he hoped she wouldn't.

When she deepened the kiss and pulled him closer, stretching one long leg out, crossing it over his, he knew she wasn't going anywhere without him tonight.

That's when what little control he had left shattered.

He eased her down onto his jacket, taking care that his touch wasn't as rough and desperate as he felt. When he covered her with his body, the only thing he was aware of was how her lips and tongue were doing amazing things to his mouth. When his hand slipped under the neckline of her dress and his fingers found their way to her breast beneath her bra, she moaned, a muffled sound under his lips.

"You okay?" he said, resting his forehead on hers. "If you want, we can stop."

* * *

She appreciated his concern. He was a gentleman, but she didn't want to talk.

She didn't want to stop, and she didn't want to talk about it.

Because if they started talking, she might try to explain herself.

She was *so tired* of explaining herself.

It was her body. Her choice to have him… Just because she chose to make love to a virtual stranger, it didn't make her any less of a human being. Men did it all the time…had one-night stands…even when they were engaged…with the church booked and the catering ordered…the white dress hanging in the bride-to-be's closet and the wedding two weeks away.

But she wasn't going to think about men like that tonight. She was going to prove to herself exactly how liberated she was. She was going to take back her power by enjoying this fine, hot guy. Her *wedding favor*. Actually, he was more like a gift…but not a wedding gift. She'd sent all those back after she'd thrown the ring in Eric's face.

She needed to *stop* thinking about Eric. He'd already ruined her life once.

There was no room for him—especially not tonight.

To drown out the incessant chatter in her head, Caitlyn deepened their kiss. Brodie groaned and nudged her thighs apart with his knee, nesting his lower body into hers. When she felt his arousal, thick and hard against her, she grabbed his backside and pulled him even closer, just to make sure there was no doubt about exactly how okay she was with their closeness.

His murmured answer was muddled and unintelligible against her lips; he seemed to understand. His intention was clear in the way he smoothed his hand up her bare leg. When his fingers reached her upper thigh and he deftly eased her out of her panties, his actions told her everything she needed to know.

When they were naked and ready, she held on tight as he unleashed himself up on her body.

Later, when they lay spent and sated in each other's arms, she wasn't sure if hours or days had passed. It was as if they'd been lifted out of space and time into a world where only the two of them existed.

But no… It couldn't have been days because it was still dark outside, and she had to go home before the sun came up. She was staying with her parents while she was here. They'd send out the National Guard if she didn't come home. She snuggled into the warmth of him for one more luxurious moment, breathing in the scent of him…of them…before she gently wriggled out from under his protective arm.

He stirred. "Where are you going?"

"I have to go home."

"Chicago? Tonight? Don't do that. Stay with me. Some of the best meteors happen just before dawn."

It was already late, but she could see her mother's face if she came in doing the walk of shame, with the sun on her back. Caitlyn may have been twenty-nine years old and living on her own since she'd gone off to college, but when she came home to visit the folks, she was twelve years old again.

"No, I'm sorry. I really do have to go."

As she straightened her clothes and smoothed her hair into place, she watched Brodie lying there, propped up on one elbow, watching her. He really was a beautiful man. That face…and that body. Oh, what he could do with that body. It was one of the best experiences she'd ever had. Not that she'd had that many. She'd certainly never done this before. Brodie the Brit had been nothing short of amazing. It was a shame that she'd never see him again. What had started out to be an evening of obligation had turned into a night she would never forget.

Never forget and definitely not regret.

"Will you walk me to my car?" she asked.

"Of course." Once he'd righted himself and brushed off the dirt from his jacket, they were walking arm in arm back to the parking lot.

"I'm sorry about your coat," she said.

"Don't give it a second thought. In fact, I might just have it framed and hang it on my wall to remember tonight."

The temperature had dropped a good ten degrees, and by the time they made it back around to the lot, most of the cars were gone. The courtesy golf carts and their drivers were nowhere to be found. It was *that* late.

As she fumbled in her purse for her keys, she checked her phone for the time.

Three forty-five in the morning.

Irrational panic ceased her. She should've been home hours ago.

She didn't want to ruin everything with awkward goodbyes, but she had to get out of there.

"Brodie the Brit," she said. They were standing maybe five inches apart. "This has been such a wonderful evening. Look, if you're ever in Chicago..."

She realized how that sounded, *a shot of needy with a chaser of desperate*.

"Goodbye, Brodie."

She kissed him one last time before she drove off.

When she did, she forced herself to not watch his fading image in her rearview mirror. Or to think about how tonight was not only her first one-night stand, it was also probably the best sex she'd ever had in her life.

The faster she drove, the louder doubt rattled behind her like a string of tin cans tied to a wedding car.

She was never going to see him again. She didn't even know his last name.

It was best that way.

Wasn't it?

Chapter Two

May

Couldn't *anything* be simple? Caitlyn Moore silently lamented.

Just once?

Apparently not, she affirmed as she listened to Jason Hallowell, head electrical engineer for Moore Entertainment, drone on about the problem.

"If Clark Ball leaves early, we will not get the work done in time to pass the electrical inspection. I'm sure I don't need to remind you, ma'am, that this will be the second time we've failed it."

No. He didn't need to remind her. The reality was an albatross, constantly following her. They were racing against the clock, and if they failed the inspection again, it would probably mean that they'd have to delay the Memorial Day soft opening of Moore Entertainment's newest theme park, Cowboy Country USA.

Caitlyn would rather eat dirt than delay the opening. She had to prove to her father that she was capable. She could pull this off despite his doubts and worries.

Even more important than proving herself, this was the one thing she could do to help her father get well. He'd suffered a massive heart attack earlier in the week, and he was under strict doctors' orders to avoid stress so that his body could heal. Caitlyn had dropped everything and flown into Lubbock from Chicago the moment she'd gotten word that he was ill. But she soon realized that sitting at his bedside wringing her hands wasn't helping anyone. That's when she decided the proactive approach would be to take a hold of the reins at Cowboy Country and make sure that the park opened as planned.

When her father heard of the plan, he'd balked and blustered—even through the tubes and the admonitions of nurses who sedated him when he wouldn't calm down. So Caitlyn did what any loving daughter would do. She told her dad that she loved him, but she wasn't coming back to see him until he promised that he could remain calm.

"Dad, I'm your best chance for making this project successful," she'd said.

"Well, that's not very good news," he'd said. "You're a beautiful girl, and I'm sure you're good at all that animal research you do, but Caitlyn, this is the real world."

"Dad, I'm not a girl. I'm twenty-nine years old, and

I'm more than capable of handling this. I mean, every-thing is in place. The park is practically ready to open its doors. I can do this. You have to trust me."

By that time the sedative was kicking in. Through heavy eyes that were threatening to close, he said, "We'll see. Make sure you keep the appointment with Hayes Consulting. They can help you. They're expensive and hard to land an appointment with. So whatever you do, keep that appointment. Janie will tell you when it is. And listen to this Hayes guy, Caitlyn. He knows what he's talking about."

With that, he drifted off to sleep. Her mother had smiled at her through watery eyes. Validation that she was doing the right thing, the only thing in her power that would allow her to take some of the pressure off her father so that he could focus on healing.

Little did she know what she was actually getting herself into. To the uninformed eye, the park may have looked like it was ready to open, but the reality was, things were a mess. As of now they hadn't passed the necessary inspections and they didn't have the permits needed to open their doors. If they didn't make the grade on this latest inspection, there was no way they'd open on time.

It was little things like this episode with Clark Ball that kept threatening to set them back.

"Jason, I'm sorry. I told Clark he could leave early today. I ran into him yesterday when I was making my rounds and he asked. I believe his wife is having medical issues. He said he needed to be there for her."

"Ms. Moore, ma'am, I'm very sorry if his wife is

sick. Truly I am. But he's been cutting out early at least once a week for the past three months. Besides, he may have asked you yesterday, but he asked me on Monday, and I told him he could not leave early today. He knows it's all hands on deck this week if we are going to get the work done."

"Are you sure there's no other way?" she asked, immediately regretting the question.

Heavy silence hung on the other end of the line. "I wouldn't be making this call if there was another way. I don't have time for this. None of us do if we're going to meet these deadlines. However, I have to say I'm disappointed that you seem to be missing the point that by asking you after I told him no, Clark has deliberately defied my authority. That's insubordination."

"I understand that, Jason, and no, it's not right. I will speak to Clark. We will come to some kind of understanding. I'm sure he will be reasonable once he understands the situation."

Again, her words were met with silence before Jason murmured a stiff, "Thank you, ma'am."

Somehow, Jason always seemed a little disappointed when he talked to her. She could offer him a fifty percent raise, and she was certain he'd greet the news with the same stony stoicism followed by and unemotional, *thank you, ma'am.*

He wasn't the only one. The crew leaders did their jobs well, but they all had a way of making Caitlyn feel as if they were simply tolerating her, as if they could see right through her bravado. Maybe she needed to give them more credit, because she wasn't at all sure that Clark Ball would be reasonable and eager to work things out. Jason had been too polite to call her bluff.

She squared her shoulders. She was the boss. Her number one objective was to make sure Cowboy Country passed all necessary inspections so they could open the park as scheduled on Memorial Day.

"Where can I find Clark right now?" she asked.

"He's supposed to be working on the wiring over at the Twin Rattlers Roller Coaster. I don't mean to tell you what to do, ma'am. But if you plan on talking to him, I wouldn't wait much longer because he says he's leaving at noon."

"Thanks, Jason. I'll head over there now. I'll let you know once I've talked to him."

"Thank you, ma'am. I'd appreciate it."

She hung up the phone and sat back in her chair for a moment. She hated being the bad guy. She really did. That's why she preferred working in the lab, doing research and development for Moore Entertainment. She was a zoologist by training, and she'd been perfectly prepared for the low entry-level salary that came with most R&D positions, but her father had hired her just out of college. Despite his reputation for being a hard-nosed, take-no-prisoners kind of businessman, he'd brought her on board. His version of the story was that he fully intended to make her fall in love with the family business. Despite her zoology degree, he intended to put her through the Alden Moore school of business, which included several years of courses like Hard Knocks and Trial by Fire.

Her father was doggedly determined that she would fall in love with the business and someday take over.

What her dear old dad didn't understand was that the research and study of animals wasn't just a passing fancy. She wanted to make it her life's work. When she graduated, she'd been hard-pressed to find a job. So when Alden offered her the job as vice president of research and development for Moore Entertainment along with a healthy salary and benefits, she'd been tempted, sure, but it was the bonus that had sealed the deal: he offered her the chance to make her dream come true. If she stayed on and helped make Cowboy Country USA a success, then there was a chance they could develop a second phase of the park, a zoo park featuring animals indigenous to Northwest Texas.

But then her father had gotten sick, and all thoughts of zoo parks and resentment for his herding her into the family business gave way to what was really important: her dad's health.

When he'd suffered a nearly fatal heart attack, she'd stepped in to make sure her father's dream didn't founder while he was fighting for his life. She'd felt so helpless when she saw him lying there in that hospital bed hooked up to all those machines. This man, who'd always been larger than life and twice as fierce, was facing a challenge that might best him. Rather than sit by his bedside wringing her hands, she vowed to step up and see Cowboy Country through the way he'd want so he could focus all his energy on getting better.

Well, in a perfect world that's what he would do, but the other side of the coin was that he had little choice but to have faith that she could pull it off. Relinquishing control would be difficult. Believing that Caitlyn was capable to lead the park through a successful opening was another matter altogether.

This was her chance to prove her worth to her father, and she intended to succeed.

She knew the longer she put off talking to Clark, the more difficult it would be. She gathered herself mentally, sat forward in her desk chair and buzzed her assistant, who was really her father's assistant. "Janie, I'm going into the park to take care of something."

"Ms. Moore, before you head out, I wanted to let you know that Mr. Hayes of Hayes Consulting is here to see you."

Oh, that's right...Hayes Consulting.

Caitlyn glanced at her watch. He was twenty minutes early. She decided to go out and greet him and then ask Janie to show him around while she put out the most recent fire. She'd only be gone thirty minutes, tops. Then she'd come back and get Mr. Hayes whatever he needed to get started with whatever it was he did to work his magic.

If she had a dime for every time her father had reinforced how important working with Hayes Consulting was to Cowboy Country, she could retire a wealthy woman. Apparently, the firm was very good at fixing the images of businesses that had managed to do something to sully their reputation. Or, as in Cowboy Country's case, had simply gotten off to a bad start in the community.

Her father had a lot of faith that this Hayes guy could

fix things. He'd underscored how expensive and difficult it was to book time with this outfit. Keeping this
meeting had been one of the few mandates her father
had given her.

"Please tell Mr. Hayes I'll be right out."

She stood and slid on her navy jacket because it was
one of the few pieces of business attire that she owned
that made her feel professional and pulled together. *Fake
it until you make it*, she told herself and strode out into
the reception area. All the blood drained from her head
when she saw Brodie the Brit—that guy from the qua-
druple Fortune wedding—standing in the middle of
the room.

"What in the world are you doing here?" She immediately regretted her tone and the words. Good grief.
Way to finesse it, Caitlyn. Or Cait. He'd only known her
as Cait. And he'd never called. So how on earth did he
find her here, two and a half months later?

For a moment, he looked as surprised to see her as
she felt, but then his handsome features hardened into a
mask so different from the way he'd looked *that night*.
His eyes were cold and guarded. Wait a minute, neither
one of them should be cold and guarded because they
were adults and they both had known what they were
getting themselves into.

"Hello, Cait," he said, offering her a hand to shake.
A hand. What was it they'd said that night at the wedding? That they were way past shaking hands. And that
was *before* they'd left the reception.

She looked at his outstretched hand but didn't shake
it. She was tempted to tell him to put that thing away,

but she should've thought of that two and a half months ago. Now she had more important things to worry about—like an employee who was about to cost them the inspection they desperately needed to open and a costly consultant who was… Speaking of… Where was he? She glanced around the waiting room. Restroom, perhaps?

His absence was a stroke of luck. She'd have time to get rid of Brodie before the situation became sticky.

"Walk with me," she said to him.

"I'd love to. However, I have an appointment."

"What a coincidence. So do I. Could you please tell me why you're here?"

He narrowed his gaze at her. "Do you work here?"

She quirked a brow at him. "You might say that. I'm not usually in this office, but my father is ill, and I'm filling in for him. Who is your appointment with?"

She watched the color drain from Brodie's formerly tanned face. "You wouldn't happen to be Cait Moore? Er…*Caitlyn* Moore?"

"The one and only."

"Fancy that. I'm Brodie Hayes, Hayes Consulting."

Caitlyn opened her mouth to say something and then closed it, because what was there to say? Nothing. Or at least nothing they could say out loud or discuss out here in the open, with Janie's eyes on them, mentally recording everything they said and did.

"Can we please go into your office?" Brodie asked.

"Not right now. I have a situation I need to take care of. You can wait for me in there, though. Make yourself comfortable, and I'll be right back. Janie, please show Mr. Hayes into my office."

"A situation?" Brodie asked.

Caitlyn glanced at her watch. She needed to hurry; she didn't want to end up chasing Clark Ball down in the parking lot. "Yes, a situation. So you'll have to excuse me."

Brodie's large body blocked her path, and when she looked up at him to send the *you need to move* message, she remembered how that body felt moving on top of her that night nearly three months ago. Heat started in her cleavage, which was modestly covered up today— as it should've been that night—and crept up her neck, spreading to her cheeks.

He crossed his arms. The body language was so defensive that she couldn't help but glance up at his face, which was stone cold and lacking any hint that he might be glad to see her.

She groaned inwardly, silently admonishing herself.

Of course he wasn't glad to see her. This wasn't a date. This was…awkward.

For God's sake, how was it that the one and only one-night stand she'd ever had in her life would turn up again—not because he'd been so smitten that he'd tracked her down. Oh, she could've handled that. But this…having him show up right now, right here. In the last place in the entire world she wanted to be reminded of her indiscretion.

"If there's a problem, I should come with you." His voice was all business. "You can brief me on the way."

She bristled, but before she demanded for a second

time that he go into her office and wait for her, she remembered he father saying Hayes Consulting was expensive and in demand. Even if he had arrived early, she had him for one afternoon, and she intended to get Moore Entertainment's money's worth.

"Okay, Brodie Hayes, if you're willing to hit the ground running. Prepare to show me what you've got."

He smirked.

Oh, God. He could take that a couple of different ways. She imagined him thinking, *honey, you've already seen everything I've got.* But that was inappropriate, and she wasn't about to let him know his appearance here today was fazing her in the least.

She turned to Janie. "Mr. Hayes and I are going out into the park. I have my cell phone if you need to get in touch with me."

Caitlyn kept walking toward the door without looking back to make sure Brodie was following her. He could keep up on his own. Plus, there was the problem that every time she looked at him, all she could think of was how he'd made love to her so thoroughly that night. There went the heat bomb, exploding in her lower parts and raising the temperature in her entire body.

Damn him.

Damn *her* for not having more self-control.

He was walking beside her now. She would not say another word about *that night*. Not on company time.

"Since I only have you for an afternoon, I'll start bringing you up to speed with all that's happening."

She dared a glance at him, if for no other reason than

to prove that she was a professional…and immune to those broad shoulders.

Stop it.

Stop thinking about shoulders.

He was looking at her as if she had two heads. It knocked any wayward thoughts of broad shoulders and meteor showers right out of her head.

"What do you mean you only have me for an afternoon? Alden Moore booked me for the entire month of May."

Bloody hell.

How could he have been so stupid to not realize what he was walking into?

Brodie prided himself on never being surprised. How had he not known his client—the client he'd worked so hard to land—the client whose business could make or break the Tokyo deal—had a daughter.

He would've never slept with her if he'd known Cait from Chicago was even remotely related to Alden Moore, much less his daughter.

Way to get off to a rocking start.

He needed to get a hold of this situation and fast, before it blew up in his face.

He drew in a deep breath to steady himself. How was he to know Cait from the wedding was *Caitlyn Moore*?

They hadn't exchanged last names. In the moment, it had seemed sexy and edgy. One night of bliss with no strings attached. Or so they'd agreed.

A few days ago, after he'd learned that Alden Moore had fallen ill and his daughter would be standing in, he'd done a cursory internet search of Caitlyn Moore, and all he'd turned up was a very private Facebook page with a profile picture of a very large dog—or maybe it was a pony?—and a dated photo with Alden Moore and a little girl who looked to be five or six. The photo looked like it was taken in the early 1990s. Nothing that would've cued him in to the fact that Cait from Chicago was not only Alden Moore's daughter, but also the executive in charge at Cowboy Country.

Still, what was done was done. His only choice now was to regroup and move past this unexpected turn of events. After all, that was how he made his living, helping people spin bad into good.

"We seem to have a miscommunication here," he said to Caitlyn as they left the office. "Your father had contracted me to work with Moore Entertainment until Cowboy Country opens successfully."

She was speed walking slightly ahead of him.

"Wonderful," she said. "Just wonderful."

"Hey, will you please stop for a moment and talk to me?"

She stopped walking so fast, he nearly ran into her. When she turned, she looked him square in the eyes. It was almost as if she were looking through him.

"Look, I need to be on the other side of the park in about five minutes to deal with a personnel issue. I don't have time to talk about what happened between us. Frankly, this isn't the time or the place. If you're going to be here for a month, I say we just move on and forget the Fortune wedding. Okay?"

The last thing he wanted to do was talk about *them*.

"That's perfectly fine with me," he said. "I give you my word of honor that I won't speak of it. Actually, what I had in mind was your briefing me on this urgent personnel issue so that I understand the situation before we arrive."

"Of course." She smiled, but it didn't reach her eyes.

As they resumed walking, past various pavilions, cowboy-themed gift shops and refreshment stands, she filled him in on Clark Ball, the employee in question.

"He deliberately defied his supervisor when he asked you for the time off," Brodie said, wanting to make sure that he understood the situation correctly.

"That's right."

"Since he's made a habit of leaving work early, has he been formally counseled about the unacceptable behavior?"

"Yes, his supervisor told me he wrote him up last week. In fact, there he is." Caitlyn nodded toward a tall, thin guy who looked to be in his early twenties. He had his keys in his hand and his cell phone pressed against his ear.

"I'll handle this, okay?"

He nodded, hanging back to watch her take care of the situation. As he watched her walk over to Ball, he couldn't help but notice the way her sensible navy blue suit hugged her in all the right places. Just like the red dress that she'd worn to the wedding. Of course, her business suit was much more conservative, but still no less tempting. He pressed his lips together, as if doing that might extinguish the attraction simmering inside him. It was the same magnetic pull that had drawn him to her the night of the wedding. The same force that had drawn him away from the twin blondes he'd been talking to before he'd glimpsed her across the room and excused himself to meet her.

Of course, everything was different now. For the next month she would be his boss, for all intents and purposes. He'd advise her on how to pull the park together in every department from staffing and personnel issues to community relations.

He watched as she stood in front of Ball, who was still talking on the phone. When Caitlyn gestured that she needed to talk to Ball, the guy turned his back on her. Something that might've qualified as primal stirred inside him. That was no way to treat a lady. It was definitely no way to treat his superior. But Brodie swallowed the urge to step in and tell the guy to get off his phone and show her some respect.

Caitlyn was being entirely too nice. He made a mental note that they'd need to talk about that. She was probably good at her job; otherwise, Alden Moore wouldn't have put her in charge while he was out. Despite the way she'd laid down the law with him a few moments ago, observing her now, he got a very strong sense that Caitlyn didn't like being the bad guy—and that her employees knew it, too.

Finally, Caitlyn tapped Ball on the shoulder. He looked a little annoyed, but he put his hand over his phone and said, "Listen, I can't talk to you now. I need to run. Remember, you told me I could leave. I'll stop into the office tomorrow and chat. How's that?"

"No, Clark, it's not all right. I said you could leave if you had your supervisor's permission."

Clark gave an oh-well shrug. "I have to pick up my brother over in Lubbock in twenty minutes. I'll be lucky to get there in half an hour. I still have to clock out and get to my car."

"You haven't clocked out and you're on a personal call?" she asked.

"Yeah, so I'll come in five minutes early tomorrow." The guy rolled his eyes as he bent to place something in his toolbox.

"Clark, when you asked for the time off, you said you needed to take your wife to an appointment. Now you're taking your brother somewhere."

This time he ignored her as he turned to walk away.

"You don't have my permission to leave," Caitlyn called out after him.

"Sorry," he called back, not even turning around. "I'll make up the time. We'll talk about it tomorrow."

Brodie had let her have a go at it; clearly it was time to step in and help her.

"Mr. Ball," he said. "I think what Ms. Moore is trying to say is if you leave, don't come back. Because you will no longer have a job here."

Chapter Three

"How dare you put words in my mouth?" Caitlyn said through gritted teeth once they were out of earshot of Clark and others who might overhear.

"I'm sorry you took it that way," Brodie said. But he didn't look one bit sorry. "Obviously, your softer approach wasn't getting through to him."

"Excuse me? What exactly do you mean by *softer approach*?" The sun was high in the sky, and she felt heat prickle the back of her neck. "Just because I didn't steamroll right over him doesn't mean I wasn't effectively handling the situation. You butted in."

"The guy was walking out the door, and you were letting him."

"*I was handling it.*" She purposely lowered her voice.

"Look, we are not going to talk about this here. Meet me in my office."

She turned and walked away without him, but he managed to catch up with her. They walked in stony silence as they made their way down Cowboy Country's Main Street, past the Foaming Barrel Root Beer Stand and Gus's General Store, to the rough-hewn wooden gate that separated the nineteenth-century cowboy town from the stark, modern Moore Entertainment executive offices.

Of course, after Brodie's sudden-death ultimatum, Clark had sullenly taken himself back to the job site. Brodie should've stayed out of it and let her do her job, rather than jumping in with both feet and a sledgehammer. She hadn't even had a chance to brief him on... anything. He didn't know what was going on or that she was completely capable of turning that situation around. She would've helped Clark see the light. He would've done the right thing in the end. She had faith in him

Apparently, Hayes Consulting was good enough to inspire her father to contract them for a month...*an entire month*. However, the Brodie Hayes of Hayes Consulting was *not* Brodie the Brit.

Was this man really the same guy who'd swept her off her feet? Because aside from his good looks and that maddeningly delicious British accent, the guy who'd presented himself today didn't resemble Brodie the Brit at all.

This guy...

Ugggh...

This guy was cocky and smug, not at all like *anyone* she'd allow to seduce her. She would never hire this guy, much less spend the better part of the night in a field, watching meteor showers and letting him put his hands all over her body…and putting her hands all over his.

The memory made her shudder…and, much to her dismay, not in a bad way. She needed to stop that right now.

She didn't slant him a glance.

From a purely objective, woman's point of view, Brodie Hayes was a handsome man, there was no debating that. But why did he have to be so disagreeable? He certainly seemed to take pleasure in pushing her buttons. Caitlyn knew his type: all flash and no substance.

A womanizer, no doubt.

But she couldn't blame him for the Valentine's Day love and dash. That was on her as much as it was on him.

Quickening her step as she approached the office, she reached out and opened the door herself, holding it for Brodie and gesturing for him to step inside first. She was no expert at office posturing and body language, but holding the door for him felt like she was putting herself back in the position of power.

Exactly where she needed to be now that everything had changed so drastically.

"Hello, Janie, we're back," she said. "Please hold calls. Oh, unless it's about my father. We're awaiting word on the latest round of tests."

Of course, her mother would probably call Caitlyn's

cell with any updates, but she just wanted to be clear…
just in case.

When Caitlyn turned around to head back into her
office, Brodie was staring at her with that same im-
passive mask he'd donned the moment they'd figured
out who was who and the mess they'd created thanks
to *that night*.

Who was this icy stoic sitting across from her? If
Brodie Hayes had acted like this, she would've left that
wedding when she should've.

"Heavy-handed threats are no way to inspire people and build a team," Caitlyn said. "Even if the team
needs some refining, they are all Cowboy Country has
right now. Electricians aren't exactly standing around
in herds. Bottom line is, that's not how we operate here.
Do you understand?"

He sat back in his chair, staring down at his hands,
which were steepled at chest level. For a moment she
thought he might apologize.

"It wasn't an easy decision for your father to hire
Hayes Consulting. Alden Moore is extremely good at
what he does. He's the amusement-park king. Hiring
me for Cowboy Country was him admitting he may
have been in a little over his head. Your dad is damn
good at what he does, but this park is a departure from
his wheelhouse. When your father hired me, one of the
first things he asked me was, 'Hayes, are you afraid to
fire people?' I assured him I wasn't."

"So what? You decided to walk in here and prove
yourself first thing, even before I could bring you up to
speed on how things work around here?"

"I didn't need to be briefed to see what that guy was about," Brodie said. "Your father has already given me my marching orders. Did he not brief you? I thought you were his second-in-command."

No, she was not his second-in-command. That would've been Bob Page. Bob had left unexpectedly after suffering critical injuries in a horseback riding accident. This happened about a week before her father's heart attack. Based on the catastrophes of Cowboy Country's number one and number two honchos, if Caitlyn didn't know better, she might've worried that this project was cursed.

She was too much of a realist for that, and she was dead set on proving to her dad that she could deliver.

"I actually work out of the research offices in Chicago."

She paused to see if he'd make any Cait from Chicago cracks.

He didn't.

She may or may not have been a little disappointed. Her rational side was relieved, but her traitorous heart, the place where she stored the snow globe memory of that night, still held out hope for some wayward spark to leap out, revealing the dashing romantic she'd met that night in February.

It didn't.

"I transferred to Horseback Hollow to take the reins while my dad is recovering."

"Yet, you don't have a copy of the briefing your dad gave me." He held up the papers.

He was so smug. She didn't know what she wanted

more: to smack that smirk off him or to walk up and kiss him to see if he could still turn her inside out.

"That's easy to fix."

Caitlyn pressed the intercom that connected her to her assistant.

"Janie, please come in here. I need you to make some copies for me."

Five minutes later, the woman was standing in front of Caitlyn with the papers.

She scanned them quickly, reading on the first page that Alden had, in fact, instructed Brodie to "slice and dice," as Alden had put it.

Slice and dice.

Get rid of anyone who didn't do the job past expectations.

She looked up. "This is how my father works. However, since he's not here, and I'm the Moore Entertainment executive in charge, you're reporting to me now. And I'm telling you, we will be making some adjustments to this plan, because it doesn't work for me. The first rule is, you don't fire anyone until you talk to me. Do you understand me?"

"Every single employee on this team needs to be *all in*. One hundred percent. If not, we won't meet our goal."

"I agree," Caitlyn said. "That also goes for the two of us working as a team and not against each other. Do you think we can do that?"

He was quiet for a moment. Their gazes were locked, but he seemed to be looking right through her.

"Of course," he said. "What's done is done. Let's put everything behind us and move forward."

For a moment she wasn't sure if he was talking about the Clark Ball incident or their Fortune wedding after-party. She certainly wasn't going to ask or let him think he could intimidate her with innuendo.

"Why don't we go walk the park? It's the best way for me to bring you up to speed. Then we can come back and figure out how we need to revise that plan, while making sure we open on time."

Brodie considered himself a go-with-the-flow kind of guy. However, when it came to business, he had one hard, fast rule: do not sleep with the clients.

It complicated matters.

He was living the reality of that truth today, and it was throwing him off his game.

He'd been blissfully unaware the night he'd met Caitlyn and had given himself over to the lure of their attraction. How could he resist? How could he have known that their worlds would collide in the most jarring way? In the years since he'd been in business, he'd never found himself in a situation like this.

After dealing with other peoples' *complicated matters* on the job all day, every day, he did his best to keep his personal life as unencumbered and hassle-free as possible. Of course, things didn't always go smoothly. He'd faced the occasional sticky wicket of finding it necessary to extract himself from the casual fling that clung too tightly. And there were uncomfortable cases when he was out with a beauty only to run into the previous evening's delight. But he prided himself on being up-front with the women in his life. Those who played by his rules stuck around for the fun of it. Those who fancied a different level of commitment usually ran out of patience and moved on.

He couldn't blame them.

In his circles, everyone knew that Brodie Fortune Hayes wasn't interested in getting serious. Work was his mistress, his lady love. He had no reserves or residual to give of himself.

As he stepped inside the Hollows Cantina, he had to ask himself if somehow he'd been able to glimpse the future and known that *Cait from Chicago* would be the person to whom he'd report at Moore Entertainment, would the night of the wedding—Valentine's Day— have taken a decidedly different turn?

His head—the place he relied on, the one voice that he always knew wouldn't steer him wrong—trumpeted a resounding *yes*. But another part of him, a place that was foreign and uncomfortable, begged to differ.

Well, then, that was easy. He was going with his head. It was the only sensible thing to do. Especially since the workday wasn't over yet.

After he and Caitlyn had wrapped the disastrous day at Cowboy Country, they'd agreed to meet for dinner at The Hollows Cantina, where they would iron out the details of their *united front* plan.

When he took the job, he'd known good and well that Alden Moore would be difficult to please. The man had a formidable reputation. Little did he know that working with Moore's daughter would prove to be even more challenging!

It went deeper than the fact that they'd seen each other naked. This woman was different from anyone he'd ever worked with. She was trying to manage a group of hostile employees with warm, fuzzy Kumbaya nonsense. She didn't seem to realize that people were walking all over her. He was willing to bet that Clark Ball wouldn't have pulled that bit of insubordinate baloney on her father. If Caitlyn Moore would simply get down from her high horse and listen to him tonight, he just might be able to help her save Cowboy Country.

First, Caitlyn had to run an errand. For that, Brodie was grateful. Her side trip took a bit of the pressure off, since that meant they were driving separately and meeting at the restaurant. Even though their dinner most definitely was not a date, taking separate cars gave them each a little breathing room to process what had transpired…*er*…on the job.

As far as he was concerned, he was putting their night under the stars behind him. In his head, *Cait from Chicago* was a different person from Caitlyn Moore, daughter of Alden Moore, the man who could make or break his chance to land the Japanese theme park account.

Brodie was used to flying solo, especially when it came to business. The companies that hired Hayes Consulting trusted him and tended to not interfere. Most had gotten themselves into messes of one kind or another, or their public profiles needed a boost. They hired him to pull them out of the bad and into a better standing in the community.

This job wasn't difficult.

Even if one might label the circumstances he dealt with…*complicated*.

He was *this close* to landing the Japanese account, and that would secure Hayes Consulting's position in the Asian market. Brodie liked to joke that the Japanese account would put him one continent closer to world domination.

It was a pretty serious joke.

When he walked into the restaurant, the hostess, a woman with long, dark hair greeted him with a bright smile.

"Good evening." Her lilting voice was bright and solicitous. "Welcome to the Hollows Cantina. How many in *your* party?"

"There will be two of us." He glanced at his watch. "I'm a little early. I'll wait in the bar until my dinner partner arrives."

"Have you dined with us before?" she asked.

"I have, but it's been a while. Since February."

"I thought you looked familiar."

Her comment gave him pause, and that's when he realized that she was looking up at him through long, dark lashes. She was an attractive woman, no doubt, but he wasn't even tempted to flirt with her. Flirting was one of his favorite sports. But he had enough sense to know that Horseback Hollow and London were worlds apart. The last thing he needed was to get himself into another romantic conundrum.

"I'll just—" He pointed toward the bar area to the left of the hostess stand and started to walk away.

"There's about a twenty-minute wait for a table," the woman said. "What's your name? I'll add it to my list."

Really? How strange, he wasn't even tempted.

Even stranger, he was relieved when Caitlyn chose that moment to enter the restaurant.

"There you are," Brodie said, realizing a little too late that he'd infused way more enthusiasm into his voice than he would have liked.

"Hello." Caitlyn cocked a brow. "Did you miss me?"

And that was another thing about her. She was cheeky. She had just enough sass to keep him from labeling her a total pushover. Probably because that sass was mostly directed at him.

The woman was a delightfully aggravating dichotomy. Just when he thought he had her figured out she pulled a U-turn and took off in the opposite direction.

"There's a bit of a wait for a table," Brodie said. "Why don't we have a drink in the bar in the meantime?"

As they turned to go, the hostess said, "If you want a table, I need a name." She tapped her list with her pen.

"Fortune Hayes," he said. "Brodie Fortune Hayes."

Caitlyn stopped. "What? You're a Fortune?"

Chapter Four

Never mind that she'd met Brodie at a Fortune wedding and that they'd skipped the last names and jumped right to the sex. Finding out this way that he was part of the illustrious Fortune clan felt like she'd discovered an enemy who'd infiltrated her family's camp.

The Fortunes were vehemently opposed to Cowboy Country because they were afraid that the park would bring in too many outsiders to Horseback Hollow and ruin the idyllic small town. Since the park meant so much to her father, Caitlyn couldn't help but take their scorn personally. Now here she was sitting at the bar with Brodie, while he perused the wine list as if the revelation of who he really was hadn't made things strange and different and even more *wrong*.

"Does my father know you're a Fortune?"

It took him a minute to look up from the leather-bound listing.

In that time, she thought about calling her dad. But then reality set in. If he didn't know, the shock would upset him. After his heart attack, he was supposed to remain as stress-free as possible. That was the whole reason she'd moved to Horseback Hollow, to steer Cowboy Country to a successful opening.

"Of course he does." He looked at her as if she'd suggested they order orange soda rather than the bottle of wine, which, given his upper-crust airs, was sure to be the best the restaurant had to offer. "Why does my being a Fortune bother you?"

Why did it bother her?

He'd done nothing to indicate he'd taken the job for nefarious reasons—to spy and report back…to whoever he'd report back to… Umm, okay, so that sounded far-fetched. But wait! What if he'd come on board to wreak sabotage to keep them from opening?

The moment the thought formed, it seemed equally ridiculous. After all, he had been the one who'd exercised tough love on Clark Ball, sending him back to work rather than letting him take the afternoon off. If Brodie wanted to sabotage them, he could've simply let the electrician walk off the job. They wouldn't have met the deadline to fix the electrical problems, and Cowboy Country would've failed the inspection.

Why *did it* bother her?

"Because it feels like you haven't been honest with me."

That seemed to wipe the smug smirk right off his face.

For about two seconds.

"*I* haven't been honest with *you*?"

She let his words hang in the air, knowing where he was going with this.

"I suppose I could say the same about you, *Cait from Chicago.*"

She refused to let his words faze her. Until he said, "Do you see how bloody ridiculous this is?"

She sighed. "Oh, my God. I do. As hard as we've tried to skirt the issue, we're going to have to talk about what happened that night."

"Well, I don't know if we have to go *that* far."

"Brodie, we do. Because if we talk about it—or at least acknowledge it—then we can move past it and get to work."

"Fair enough. We had sex and it was quite wonderful, if you must know."

She felt her face flush. "Well, I really wasn't thinking we should editorialize, but thank you."

Dammit, it had been good. One night of pure pleasure that would've been pretty darn-near close to perfect if he hadn't reappeared in her life and reignited that longing she felt every time she looked at him…or caught him looking at her…like he was doing right now.

But if this—this partnership—was going to work… "It can't happen again."

"I know."

Even though it went against everything she knew was right, the thought of not touching him, of him not touching her, made her heart hurt.

But why? For what?

"We have to be a team, Brodie. A platonic team."

He nodded, but the way he was looking at her sort of canceled out the word *platonic*, and she wished she could recant that part. But she couldn't. They had work to do. She couldn't let her father down because her mind was occupied with a man who had one-night stands and was perfectly content—no, he wasn't just content, he preferred to not see the woman again.

Until him, she'd never done that before. She'd had one serious relationship, and she would've married the guy if he hadn't cheated.

No, she and Brodie Fortune Hayes were too different. Clearly, they approached business and love from two opposing perspectives.

"We have to be on the same page."

He nodded again.

Stop looking at me like that.

"Absolutely," he agreed. "Why don't we start by picking out a bottle of wine and then we can talk specifics."

The wine helped. It loosened them up enough so they could start talking plans and strategies. It probably helped to talk about the ten-ton elephant that had been standing between them, Caitlyn thought as she walked with Brodie down Main Street later that week, looking at all the crafts and food booths set up for the inaugural Horseback Hollow Arts and Crafts Festival, an event created by the Fortune Foundation to reinforce Horseback Hollow's sense of community. It was clear that the two of them had very different ideas of how to turn Cowboy Country around in the weeks before the soft opening.

She knew he was a professional and darn good at what he did. He'd have to be for her father to hire him. But she couldn't help her gut feeling that his slice-and-dice approach—one that utilized fear and an iron fist to push people into place—just wasn't right.

Most of the workers were Horseback Hollow locals who needed the jobs Cowboy Country USA was providing. Clearly, some of them were torn, possibly feeling like traitors to the community. Caitlyn had reminded Brodie more than once that this unrest was due in large part to his relatives taking such a negative stand against the amusement park.

"How can they do that when they don't really know us?" she'd asked after they'd been seated for dinner at a table upstairs on the Cantina's open-air terrace.

He'd maintained that she couldn't manage by gut feelings. That his tactics had a track record and were proven to work. Just when she started to consider the evening a stalemate, he finally hit on something that allowed them to climb to middle ground.

"You said the folks of Horseback Hollow don't know Cowboy Country and what you're all about," he said. "Have you gotten out into the community to meet people?"

She'd blinked at him.

"I've been here less than a week, Brodie, and part of that time was spent at the hospital in Lubbock with my father."

"That sounds like an excuse to me." He said the words with such a straight face she searched his gaze to see if he was kidding. As usual, she couldn't tell.

"Are you kidding? Because if not, that's really harsh. That's exactly the kind of attitude I'm having a difficult time with."

He'd reached out and put his hand on her arm and darned if her traitorous body didn't zing all the way down to her toes, and some very private places perked up at the memory of his touch.

"I'm sorry," he said. "I don't mean to come across as heartless—"

She pulled her hand away, reclaiming her space and willing the humming in her body to go away. "Well, then stop saying heartless things. And if you tell me that you don't have a heart—again—I just might have to spill my wine in your lap."

He held up his hand as if to fend her off. "I'm very sorry your dad is ill, but the reality is the clock doesn't stop. Time is ticking whether or not you have good reasons for not doing everything in your power every single day to fix what's wrong with Cowboy Country. I'm here to help you, but you're going to have to let me help you."

"I appreciate your expertise," she said. "However, I can't stand by your philosophy of coming in and firing the locals. That's not going to win us many friends. Except maybe to the staffing agency we'll have to use to ensure we have enough warm bodies for opening day. How loyal do you think temps will be? Then if you start importing people from Lubbock, that'll simply compound the town's resentment. Not only have we fired the locals, we've given those jobs to people from out of town."

They'd studied the menus in silence for a long time before Brodie finally said, "I have an idea. When I was downtown, I saw a poster that said the Horseback Hollow Arts and Crafts Festival starts on Friday. Let's go have a look. That would be one of the best ways to get out in the town and get a feel for who you're dealing with. Maybe even meet some people who can give you some perspective."

It was the first idea he'd offered that she could get on board with. So here they were in the middle of Main Street. She felt as anonymous as she had at the wedding. At least the town was large enough that she wasn't conspicuous.

They strolled along together, and Caitlyn tried to ignore how they probably looked like a couple walking by booth after booth—a stand of bright watercolors; another one offering gorgeous quilts; others proudly displaying hand-thrown pottery, free-form sculpture and delicate orchids that were apparently crafted out of clay and looked more alive than the real deal.

Just as they passed the clay flowers, Caitlyn had the feeling someone was watching her. She looked across the street and locked eyes with a lady standing at the cotton-candy vendor. The stylish woman, who looked to be in her late fifties, maybe her early sixties, had silver hair cut into a smart, chic bob. Even at a glance, she had an air of class and elegance.

The woman held Caitlyn's gaze a little longer than what might be considered a casual coincidence. Just as Caitlyn began to fear that she'd somehow recognized her as part of the Cowboy Country crew, the woman ducked into the crowd and disappeared.

She was so put together, Caitlyn hated to admit that she seemed a bit more stylish than the typical woman of Horseback Hollow... Oh, that wasn't fair. Who was she to judge?

The woman was probably one of the artists. Maybe she'd seen her in one of the booths they'd passed earlier.

Then again, maybe she was a local who'd gone to rally her neighbors with their torches and pitchforks. And that was the craziest thought yet. If she was going to get to know the locals, she'd inevitably have to have that first uncomfortable moment when they discovered who she was. But then she'd be on the right track to showing them she and Moore Entertainment fully intended to be good neighbors.

She didn't say anything to Brodie, who seemed to be unaware as the two of them walked, talking and taking in the lay of the land, getting a sense of the cute little town and people who'd come to display their wares. Each booth sported a tag with the artist's name, art medium and hometown. Caitlyn was surprised to see how many of them were not local.

"So I'm guessing the good folks of Horseback Hollow support the arts and crafts festival because it's not permanent?" Caitlyn asked. "I'm intrigued that so many of the artists are from places other than here."

Brodie nodded. "Well, you have to consider that it's a small town, and there's a relatively small number of artists. Or at least ones who are good enough to win a place in the festival. From what I understand, this show is by invitation only, and it's quite an honor to be selected to participate. In other words, Horseback Hollow doesn't discriminate when it comes to discriminating."

Hmm… Obviously.

Finally, a booth manned by a local caught Caitlyn's eye: Susie's Silverworks.

"Wait," Caitlyn said. "I want to go in here."

Brodie scanned the booth, and she saw his eyes virtually glaze over.

"While you're having a look," he said, "if you'll excuse me, I'm going to go return a phone call. It shouldn't take long. Shall I meet you here when I'm done? That way you won't have to rush."

"I take it sterling-silver jewelry isn't your thing?" Caitlyn teased.

"No, I'm more of a chunky golden chain kind of guy, myself." He gave her that sexy half smile, and suddenly she was picturing him with his shirt open—not in a smarmy 1970s lounge lizard way. In fact, gold chains didn't even figure in her mind's picture.

And she needed to stop that—

"You are the golden boy, aren't you?"

He shot her a look that implied she didn't know what she was talking about. "I'll see you in a few minutes."

Caitlyn waited until two browsers had finished looking and moved over so she could take their spot. Then she could see that Susie offered a gorgeous array of handcrafted jewelry—rings, earrings, necklaces and free-form charms. But it was the tray of hammered silver cuff bracelets that caught her eye.

"Are you Susie?"

The woman nodded. "I am. These are my creations."

"They're beautiful."

"Thank you." Susie beamed at her. "Please, try on anything you'd like."

"Oh, I love this one." Caitlyn pointed to a concave hammered silver cuff with beveled edges. Susie picked it up and polished it with a velvety black cloth before she offered it to Caitlyn.

"May I?" Susie nodded toward Caitlyn's wrist.

"Please." She held out her arm and allowed the artist to slip on the bracelet.

"What do you think?"

"I think I'm in love," Caitlyn said.

Out of the corner of her eye, she glimpsed that silver-haired woman again. The one she'd caught staring at her and Brodie as they'd wound their way through the crowd down Main Street. This time there was no doubt. The woman was watching her from the next booth. In fact, she was craning her neck.

Caitlyn smiled at her. The woman smiled back. But a knot of people meandered through their line of vision, and by the time they'd moved on, the woman was gone.

At least she'd smiled, which was a good indication that she hadn't summoned the angry mobs. But the woman's attention did make Caitlyn squirm a little bit. Probably because she spent so much time alone in her research. In a city the size of Chicago, it was easy to be alone in a crowd. She saw some of the same faces on her walk to and from her office, but she never connected with any of them. Maybe it was the city girl in her that made her feel suspicious of a smile. When she thought of it that way, suspicion didn't feel right, either.

"Try this one." Susie held up another cuff bracelet. This one was smooth and shiny and about half the width of the other one. Caitlyn removed the first bracelet from her wrist and put on the one Susie offered in its place.

"This one is beautiful, too."

"If you want something a little less dressy, I have these."

She placed five silver bangles on a black velvet pad she'd set atop the glass case. Some of them had inlaid stones; others were plain.

"And here are the matching earrings."

Caitlyn sighed. "It's all so pretty, but I think I prefer the cuff bracelets. Now, for the difficult decision. Which one?"

"Try them both on," Susie urged.

Caitlyn slipped one onto each wrist and held out her arms to admire and compare the two pieces of jewelry.

"I vote for the hammered silver," said a female voice behind Caitlyn.

When she turned around, she saw the woman with the silver hair. She held up her own arm, showing off a cuff similar to the one Caitlyn was partial to, but it was just different enough to make each piece unique.

"She has good taste," the woman said to Susie.

"She certainly does," Susie agreed. "How are you, Jeanne Marie? I was wondering when you were going to stop by and see me."

Susie turned to Caitlyn. "Jeanne Marie is one of my best customers."

"Please don't tell that to my husband," she said.

She turned to Caitlyn. "Have we met? You look very familiar."

So that was the reason the woman had been staring. Of course. It made Caitlyn feel better knowing she was simply trying to place her.

"I don't believe we have. I'm Caitlyn Moore."

Caitlyn offered her hand. The woman accepted it.

"Nice to meet you, Ms. Moore. Are you a Horseback Hollow resident, or are you just here for the art festival?"

"I recently moved to the area," Caitlyn said.

"Is that so? What brought you here?"

Caitlyn took a deep breath. Her mission today was to reach out to the people in the community. Jeanne Marie seemed like a great person to start with.

"My job brought me here. I'm with Cowboy Country USA. I've come to town to help open the park."

In a split second the air seemed to change, to chill. Jeanne Marie and Susie glanced at each other and then back at Caitlyn. Jeanne Marie raised her chin and tilted her head to the right as she conjured a polite smile that didn't reach her eyes.

Caitlyn removed the cuffs from her wrists and set them on the piece of velvet.

"Susie, I'll take the hammered silver bracelet." She pulled her wallet out of her purse.

"That's a good choice," Jeanne Marie said, her voice proper and chilly.

Caitlyn tried to think of something clever to say or some way to spin this situation—where was Brodie when she needed him?—but only the truth felt right. It was all she had to offer.

"Jeanne Marie, I haven't been in Horseback Hollow very long, but I already love this town. I love the way everyone here looks out for their neighbors. They only want what is best for the community. I understand why people might be a bit skeptical about a place like Cowboy Country USA. You're probably afraid that it won't fit into the fabric of your close-knit community. But if you'll just give us a chance, I assure you, we want to be good neighbors."

Jeanne Marie's polite smile didn't waver, but it wasn't any warmer, either. Obviously, she wasn't convinced.

"I appreciate you saying that. You seem very sincere. However, I'm more interested in hearing how you are acquainted with my nephew, Brodie Fortune Hayes."

It took Brodie a little longer than he'd intended to take care of his phone call. He was half expecting Caitlyn to have moved on from the jewelry tent where he'd promised to meet her. But there she was.

Even in the midst of a crowd, his eyes picked her out, the same way he had at the wedding. With her long, dark hair and ivory skin, the woman was a stunner. Her warm heart and ready smile made her even more beautiful. What man in his right mind wouldn't find her attractive?

However, his appreciation was derailed when he realized she was talking to his aunt Jeanne Marie.

Uttering a choice word under his breath, he quickened his pace. This was not good. Not good at all.

"Hello, Auntie." He planted a kiss on the woman's cheek. "It's a lovely day for an art festival, right? I see you've met my friend, Caitlyn."

"Yes, I have, dear." Jeanne Marie's lips thinned as she secured Brodie with her gaze. "I understand congratulations are in order. Ms. Moore was telling me that the two of you are working together. I didn't realize you had landed the Cowboy Country account. In fact, I'd wager that our entire family will be just as surprised as I."

Surprised being the operative word. It was clear that she wasn't happy for him. He should have told her that was the reason he'd come back to Horseback Hollow. Or he should've at least confided in his mother or his brother Oliver. Of course, his mother would have, no doubt, shared the news with the rest of the family.

Bloody hell, now he'd stepped in it deep.

He'd been busy, and frankly, he knew how his family felt about Cowboy Country USA, and didn't want them to deliberate on the merit of his client. In the past, they had never taken an interest in his client list. Why should they get involved now?

He knew this spelled trouble. He needed to fix it.

And fast.

"Ah, well, Caitlyn, dear, you spoiled my big announcement."

Caitlyn shot him a don't-you-dare-try-to-blame-this-on-me look. His only defense was to redirect and redouble his efforts toward his aunt.

"I was going to tell everyone at the barbecue tomorrow night. May I trust you to keep my secret? It would be such a shame to spoil the surprise for everyone else."

Jeanne Marie sighed and shook her head.

He turned back to Caitlyn. "My aunt Jeanne Marie and uncle Deke throw the best barbecues you've ever seen in your life. No one does authentic Texas barbecue the way they do. The best you've *ever* seen."

He was speaking the truth, even if he was laying it on a little thick.

"Auntie, I was serious when I said I wanted to tell everyone at the barbecue tomorrow. Will you please keep this revelation between us until I have a chance to make my announcement?"

The woman didn't suffer fools lightly. She knew when she was being played, even if that wasn't his intention. She had backed him into a corner. It was his only available move.

Jeanne Marie put her hands on her slim hips. "I'll tell you what, Brodie. I will let you break the news to the family on one condition."

"Sure, what would that be?"

"I would like for you to bring Caitlyn to the barbecue. I think she might do a better job of helping you win the family over for Cowboy Country USA than you will explaining yourself on your own."

Chapter Five

Caitlyn Moore was better at charming his family than he was, Brodie thought as he pulled open the door to the rehabilitation center in Lubbock where Alden Moore was convalescing.

It shouldn't come as a surprise. She was passionate about Cowboy Country, well-spoken and beautiful. Oh, yes, she was a beauty, Caitlyn Moore—with her long, dark hair, green eyes and that flawless face of fine-boned porcelain.

She was the type of woman who haunted a man's dreams, the type who inspired a guy to cross the room to meet her. Once he got there, he realized she was so much more than a pretty face.

That *so much more* was the reason her mixing with his family was a problem.

He'd been ruminating on it for the past two days since his aunt Jeanne Marie had invited Caitlyn to the family barbecue. Brodie knew winning over the locals was crucial to improving Cowboy Country's profile, but accomplishing this through his family wasn't the route he wanted to take. He needed to keep work and family separate.

While he'd been blessed with this new group of close-knit relations, beneath the surface, everything was not as bright and shiny and perfect as it appeared.

Make no mistake, he adored his mother. He had nothing but the deepest respect for his late stepfather, Sir Simon Chesterfield. After all, the man had raised him as one of his own. In fact, he was the only father figure in Brodie's life. He and his natural brother, Oliver, understood each other because they were cut from the same cloth—literally. Oliver and Brodie were spawns of their mother's first marriage to Rhys Henry Hayes, an abominable man who was best forgotten. A man who abandoned his wife and turned his back on his children because he didn't deserve the energy that it would take to hold a grudge.

Then there was the matter of the Fortunes. His relationship with his extended family was complicated.

A couple of years ago, his mother had discovered she had been adopted when she was very young—too young to even remember—and was reunited with her American siblings, one of whom was none other than James Marshall Fortune, the American business tycoon. All of a sudden she had a branch of American family. Actually, the Fortune side of the family was more like an entire forest than a branch due to the vast number of them. There seemed to be a Fortune on every corner in Horseback Hollow.

His mother had enthusiastically embraced her new family, and she had expected her children to follow suit. Out of respect to Josephine, Brodie had taken the Fortune name when his mother had asked her children to do so.

Sometimes when Brodie Fortune Hayes was alone with his deepest, darkest thoughts, he mused that bearing the surnames of a man who had made it perfectly clear he did not want to be a father and a clan he really didn't even know, was it any wonder he didn't feel as if he had a genuine place in this world?

When he felt himself sliding down that slippery slope, he redoubled his focus on work and his determination to succeed. He was a self-made man, after all. He had built Hayes Consulting from the ground up, with no help from anyone.

That was his place, his identity, his armor.

Even though he cared deeply for his family, sometimes their enthusiasm only complicated things.

They were human. Humans were fickle and self-serving. In this dog-eat-dog world, when it came down to it, wasn't everyone out for himself?

For what other reason would salt-of-the-earth Jeanne Marie mean to interfere in his business? He didn't need to ask her permission. That's why he wasn't keen to elaborate on the reason that had brought him to Horseback Hollow.

Family could get inside your head, under your skin

and cause you to second-guess yourself. They could change everything, and they didn't always have your best interest at heart. He'd let that happen once. *Once.* Now he subscribed to the theory *Fool me once shame on you, fool me twice—* Well, that would simply make him a jackass.

Businessmen like Alden Moore didn't hire jackasses.

The rehabilitation center was nicer than some private clubs Brodie had visited. An attractive young woman greeted him from a polished dark wood desk in the center of the marble entryway.

"Good morning, sir, how may I help you?"

"I'm here to see Alden Moore. He's expecting me."

The woman typed something into a computer and then picked up the telephone.

"Your name, sir?"

"Hayes. Brodie Fortune Hayes."

It still felt odd including Fortune in his name, but if there was any place in the world that he could get mileage out of it, surely it was in Texas. He might as well take advantage of it.

As the woman murmured something into the telephone receiver, Brodie glanced around the posh surroundings. The place looked new, with its high ceilings lined with crown molding and large windows that let in just enough light to show off the Persian rugs and expensive-looking furniture. Not that he'd had the occasion to visit many rehab centers, but this one seemed more like a luxury hotel. It also allowed him to glimpse the type of service Alden Moore expected. He would get nothing less from Hayes Consulting.

"Mr. Moore is expecting you. You may go on back. He's in room 222. Take the elevator up to the second floor and follow the posted signs."

The luxury didn't stop at the reception desk. The elevator also had marble floors. It carried him to the second level where tasteful artwork adorned walls with wainscoting. Alden Moore's room was at the very end of the hall. The door was shut, just slightly ajar, as if someone had just left. Brodie knocked and pushed it open a hair.

"Brodie Hayes, my man," said Moore. "Come in, please."

The last time Brodie saw Alden, the man had been the picture of robust health. It was shocking to see him lying in a hospital bed hooked up to tubes and machines. He knew Alden wouldn't want his pity, so he made sure to keep his face neutral.

An elegant older woman with dark hair pulled back away from her face and beautiful green eyes sat in a leather chair at his bedside. Brodie had a vision of what Caitlyn might look like in about twenty-five years. Something flared in his chest for the briefest second, before he got a hold of himself.

Alden Moore introduced his wife, Barbara. After a moment of polite small talk, Barbara excused herself.

"It's nice to meet you, Mr. Hayes. I'll leave you and Alden alone to talk business. I'm trusting that you will keep things light and short. My husband is still recovering. He's not supposed to get upset about anything."

She smiled at Brodie, and he understood where Caitlyn got her quiet strength.

"Of course," he said. "I've simply come to update him on the progress Caitlyn and I have made. No upsetting news to share."

Unless you counted the fact that three months ago he'd had a one-night stand with their daughter. Brodie did not kiss and tell, so that was not even on the agenda. However, it struck him hard… He had slept with the man's *daughter*, and it just didn't feel right.

Well, actually, it had felt right. It had felt better and more natural than just about any other sexual experience he'd had. He and Caitlyn had been two consenting adults who had entered into their night of passion willingly—enthusiastically—but standing here in front of her father, it felt wrong. Until this very moment he hadn't given much thought to having a family. However, if someday he had a daughter like Caitlyn, any guy who disrespected her in any way would have a hefty price to pay.

"How is everything? What have you and that daughter of mine been up to?"

Reflexively, Brodie wanted to say, *nothing*. But he knew that was simply his guilty conscience speaking. Brodie knew Alden was speaking in terms of business.

"What progress have you made?" Moore continued.

"We are working together well."

"I'm sorry I didn't have a chance to brief you on my situation before you arrived." Moore gestured to his chest. "This was a bit unexpected, as you can imagine. I appreciate you being so flexible and willing to work with Caitlyn."

"It's not a problem, sir. In fact, we make a good team

because she sees things from a different perspective than I do."

Alden surprised Brodie by waving off his words. "I'll be honest with you. Caitlyn is at Cowboy Country because it's where she feels like she's doing the most good. There wasn't enough room for two women to sit by my bedside wringing their hands. So when she came up with the idea of working at the park while I recovered, frankly, I was in no physical condition to protest. As long as she's not in the way—not keeping you from getting the job done—just work around her."

Brodie didn't know what to say. He and Caitlyn certainly didn't see eye to eye, but she did have some good ideas. He was sincere when he said they balanced each other.

"Or if you feel you can work better without her there, I'll have her mother talk her into going back to Chicago," Alden continued. "Obviously, I'm out of danger. There's no sense in her hanging around. She'd probably be happier going back to her animal research."

Brodie was weighing his words, looking for the right response when he looked up and saw Caitlyn standing in the doorway holding a large vase of flowers.

"Excuse me?" Caitlyn said. She'd always heard the expression *seeing red*, but this was the first time she'd experienced it. She took a deep breath before she said anything else, because she knew her father's condition was serious, and fighting was the last thing he needed— even if he'd just marginalized her and hurt her as she'd never been hurt in her life. Not even when she was in college and he'd tried to talk her out of majoring in zo-ology. Not even when he'd told her it was a worthless degree and she'd be wasting her time and his money. Not even when he'd created the research position for her and she'd had to endure his barbs about that job being the only place she would be able to earn a decent wage.

Now he was telling Brodie Fortune Hayes that she was extraneous? That she could simply be shipped off and put back in her office in Chicago if she were *in the way*?

"Ahh, there she is," her father said, as if she'd walked in and overheard them singing her praises.

She pinned Brodie with a pointed look.

But she looked at her father—really looked at him. He looked much smaller, almost frail, lying there in that hospital bed with all those tubes stuck in his body and all the blinking and beeping machines registering his vitals. Dear God, he'd suffered a massive heart attack. He'd undergone major surgery not even two weeks ago.

He could've died.

That was the tipping point. The reality.

When it came down to it, family was the only thing that mattered.

The best way to prove that she wasn't simply his lit-tle princess who could be dismissed and kept *out of the way* was to prove that she was strong enough to handle even the toughest situations.

Situations like this.

She let the hurtful words roll off her and mustered her bravest smile. "I'm so sorry I'm late for the meeting. Maybe next time you'll let me know. How are you feeling, Dad? These are for you."

She placed the vase on his nightstand and leaned down to kiss him on the forehead.

"I'm fine. Just fine. In fact, as soon as I can get the nurses to unhook me from these contraptions, I'll go start training for a triathlon. Can you think of a better way to test the improvements being made to my old ticker?"

He laughed, but it sounded so hollow and sad to Caitlyn.

"Are you behaving yourself for the nurses?" she asked.

He waved her off. "What fun would that be? But Caitlyn, Brodie and I were just talking about Cowboy Country. Since I am on the mend, there's really no reason for you to stay in Horseback Hollow. It sounds like Brodie has everything under control. If you want to go back to Chicago, he can work with the staff we have in place to get the park up and running. That way you won't have to be inconvenienced."

"Inconvenienced? Is that what you think? Because it couldn't be further from the truth. I really want to stay."

Caitlyn took extra care to keep her tone light yet businesslike. She wasn't going to spar with him, even though verbal jousting sometimes seemed like their language of love.

And she refused to look at Brodie, even though she could feel his gaze on her—staring right through her, boring a hole with those maddeningly blue eyes.

It wasn't fair that one man could be so attractive and

such a double-crossing rat fink. Stronger words came to mind, actually. But she refused to lose control.

He was good at that—making her lose control—but she wasn't going to think about that right now. If she knew what was good for her she wouldn't think about it ever again.

"I thought you would be eager to get back to your research," her father said.

"Sir, if you don't mind my saying so, I could use Caitlyn's help. We're a good team."

She did a double take to make sure she was hearing him right.

She had. Apparently.

What was he up to? He even had the audacity to look sincere.

She had to bite her tongue to keep from telling her father the reason she didn't want to leave was because if Brodie were left to his own devices, they wouldn't be able to open because he would probably fire the entire Cowboy Country workforce.

How would he explain that to his Fortune family? Better yet, how would the Fortunes explain to the community that it was one of their own who had taken jobs away from the locals and given them to people from Lubbock or God only knew where else?

But she doubted her father would have much sympathy for a guy like Clark Ball.

It dawned on her that Brodie and her father were cut from a similar cloth. She was the lone wolf here. But she would stand her ground.

Her gut told her she could prove to the citizens of

Horseback Hollow that Cowboy Country USA and Moore Entertainment would be good neighbors.

She would start proving that at the Fortune barbecue on Friday night.

"Dad, Brodie and I do bring different strengths to the table. So don't worry about Cowboy Country. We have it under control. We will open the park on time. I promise."

Her dad didn't argue. That, more than anything, worried her. As he lay there in a hospital bed, he didn't seem to have any fight in him.

"Okay," he said. "I will leave it to the two of you."

The door opened. "Caitlyn, darling, I didn't realize you were here."

Her mother walked over and enfolded her in a hug.

"Hi, Mom. Have you met Brodie?"

Her mother smiled her gracious smile. "Yes. We met a few moments ago. As happy as I am to see you, I am afraid the two of you will have to leave because your father needs his rest."

When Caitlyn glanced back at her dad, he was lying there with his eyes closed.

Barbara walked Brodie and Caitlyn to the door and ushered them out into the hallway. She pulled the door closed, but took care so that it didn't make noise.

"May I bring you anything, Mom?"

Her mother had been practically living at the rehabilitation center since Caitlyn's father had been released from the hospital. She hadn't felt up to the task of caring for her husband on her own in these critical postsurgical days, but that didn't mean she wasn't attentive.

She spent every waking moment with him, only going home to sleep. And those brief breaks had only come after she was sure he was stable.

"No, thank you, sweetheart. It's so nice of you to offer, but I have everything I need right here. They bring me a dinner tray when they bring your father's. The food here is delicious. I know, who would've thought? But that was one of the criteria on your father's list before he would agree to come here. You know how he is about his food. I'm just glad he has agreed to change some of his ways so that the triple bypass will take. The doctor warned him that surgery alone would not be enough. He needed to make some major lifestyle adjustments."

Tears welled her mother's green eyes, and Caitlyn reached out and took her hand. Brodie was uncharacteristically quiet, standing there observing.

"Are you taking care of yourself, Mom? That's important."

She waved away Caitlyn's words with the flutter of her manicured hand and swiped at her tears. "Oh, I'm sorry for being so silly. Look at me. Well, actually, no, don't look at me." She laughed and Caitlyn did, too. Brodie maintained his stony silence.

"I'm sure the two of you have better things to do," she said sweetly. "You two go ahead and get out of here. Go get some lunch or go take care of business. Whatever it is, thank you both for taking the worry off Alden. It's such a blessing to have the two of you to count on."

Caitlyn hugged her mother.

"I love you, sweetheart," she said. She pulled away

then turned to Brodie and took his hand. "I just met you, but clearly Alden trusts you to run the business—and with Caitlyn, of course. And if Caitlyn thinks enough of you to work with you, you must be a fine young man."

"Thank you for saying that, Mrs. Moore. We make a good team."

They said their goodbyes. The two of them were quiet as they waited for the elevator.

It was slowly sinking in that Brodie had not only stood up for her, but he had also admitted that they each brought qualities to the job that complemented each other.

She had a flashback of the night they met and how they had complemented each other as they lay together under the stars. The memory was visceral, and she felt it all the way down to her toes.

When the elevator dinged and the doors opened, she realized that night was in the past. If she knew what was good for her, good for Cowboy Country, she would leave it there and leave those feelings alone.

She stole a glance at Brodie, remembering how good he had been to her father. In fact, the demeanor of the man she glimpsed talking to her father was closer to the Brodie who'd swept her off her feet the night of the wedding.

Which Brodie was real? The Brodie of that night or the one who had burst onto the scene at Cowboy Country? Or did it really matter?

Somewhere along the way someone had persuaded him he didn't have a heart. Despite his bravado, her instincts told her that wasn't true. Who had hurt him? Who had convinced him he was heartless?

She intended to find out and help Brodie see that holding a grudge didn't change the past, it simply clouded the future.

Chapter Six

The following Friday, Brodie arrived at Jeanne Marie and Deke's ranch a few minutes before people were due to start showing up at the barbecue. He had assured Caitlyn it was okay if she wanted to bow out of the dinner. He would've bowed out if it wouldn't have created an international incident.

With or without Caitlyn in attendance this evening, Brodie planned on telling the family Cowboy Country USA was his newest client and the reason he'd come back to Horseback Hollow.

In his line of work, he'd learned that it was all in the presentation. He wasn't there to ask their permission, because it certainly wasn't up for discussion. So he was simply going to mention it in a matter-of-fact way and remind everyone about the economic benefits that Cowboy Country could offer this tiny Texas town.

After all, his sister-in-law-to-be, Amber Rogers, was set to star in the park's Wild West Show, and Horseback Hollow wasn't the first small town to coexist with an outfit like Cowboy Country. Their presence certainly didn't spell imminent demise.

He didn't want to get that heavy-handed, and he hoped they wouldn't make it come to that, but he was prepared, just in case. Best-case scenario would be that he mentioned it, and the party went on as usual. He would certainly steer the conversation that way. He would remain in control of the situation, and everything would work out fine.

He parked his rented BMW next to a line of three pickup trucks and a large SUV. Noting his brother Oliver's car among the bunch, he grimaced, wishing he'd just confided in Oliver before breaking the news to the family as a whole. For moral support, if nothing else.

Ah, well. He was used to dealing with greater setbacks—if you could even call that a setback. Poor planning was his own fault.

Brodie grabbed the bottle of red wine and bouquet of spring flowers he had picked up at the superette on the way through town. His mother had taught him that one should never show up to a dinner party empty-handed. He supposed a backyard barbecue counted as a dinner party. Better to be safe than rude.

When he got out of the car, the first thing that hit him was the delicious smell of barbecue. His stomach rumbled, and he realized he was starving. He had to admit one of the things he had grown genuinely fond of in the United States was Texas barbecue.

As if his heart had a mind of its own, it wanted to add Caitlyn Moore to that best-loved list, too. Perhaps he was feeling more protective than fond... But were those feelings mutual?

Blinking away the thought, he let himself in the front door.

He still felt funny about not knocking, but the first time he had announced himself rather than just walking in, he'd had to endure a lecture about *family never closing their doors to family*. He was sternly reminded he was family and he was to simply let himself in, no matter what.

As if that made him feel more welcome.

They really didn't understand, did they? While his mum and stepfather, Simon, had been very good to him and his siblings, they had grown up in boarding schools and had spent many of their holidays away from their relations. This *one-big-happy-family, what's-mine-is-yours, no walls—or doors—*mentality was hard for him to digest even if his mum had adopted it wholeheartedly. For that matter, his half sister, Amelia, had come to Horseback Hollow for another Fortune wedding about a year ago, and had fallen in love with and married Quinn Drummond, a real-life cowboy. And of course, his brother Oliver was married to Shannon Singleton, a local woman he'd hired as nanny for his toddler son.

It was frightening. His family seemed to be taking to Horseback Hollow like rodeo riders to bulls. And then he inhaled more delicious smells coming from the kitchen and forgot everything except that he was famished, and the food for this dinner party—er, barbecue—smelled divine.

He followed his nose and the voices coming from the kitchen, where the unmistakable lilt of his mother's British accent contrasted with the gentle, down-home twang of his aunt's Texas drawl.

"Hello," he said as he stepped through the kitchen door.

"Brodie!" The two women greeted him with such enthusiasm it brought a smile to his lips. His aunt showed no signs of animosity or hints that she had spilled the beans about his association with Cowboy Country. He had to admit that his aunt was a good woman who could be trusted to keep her word. A twinge of remorse bit at him for doubting her.

"These are for you." He held out the wine and flowers.

"How sweet of you, darling," Jeanne Marie said. "Thank you."

As she took a large crystal vase down from one of the cupboards, she said over her shoulder, "Where is your *friend* Caitlyn?"

Her emphasis on the word *friend* didn't escape him. Neither did the glance that his aunt and his mother shared. Obviously, they had talked. Maybe he'd given Jeanne Marie too much credit too soon.

"Who is this Caitlyn?" His mother's blue eyes shone brightly. "I understand she's very pretty."

So they *had* talked.

Perhaps rather than waiting to tell the family as a

whole, it was better to nip this in the bud. Besides, whether or not Jeanne Marie had realized it, she'd just presented the perfect opportunity for him to casually talk about his association with Cowboy Country.

"It sounds like you already know quite a bit about her." Brodie cast a pointed look at his aunt. "Yes, she is exceptionally pretty."

"Why didn't you pick her up, like a gentleman would?" His mom frowned at him down her perfect aquiline nose.

"As I was trying to say, this is not a date. Caitlyn and I are purely platonic, Mum. We're work associates. Caitlyn Moore's family owns Cowboy Country USA, that amusement park they're building over off Buchanan Highway. Moore Entertainment hired Hayes Consulting to help with the opening because it seems that the majority of the people of Horseback Hollow have preconceived notions and have already made up their minds that pumping dollars into the local economy is a bad thing. I don't understand that kind of thinking, and I am happy to help them get off on a better foot."

The two women stared at him as if he had just slapped them. He supposed in a way he had. His words had come out harsher than he had intended, but sometimes it took a verbal slap to dislodge preconceived notions.

Still, he hated the thought of hurting either of them. Perhaps he had come on a little too strong. He knew Caitlyn would have certainly thought so.

Since she would be arriving shortly, he didn't want

to have poisoned the two matriarchs of the Fortune family against her.

"That sounded a little strong, and I apologize. If anyone was able to keep an open mind and consider the good that Moore Entertainment is bringing to Horseback Hollow, I know it would be the two of you. Auntie, you met Caitlyn. You spoke with her. You liked her well enough to invite her into your home even after you knew she was with Cowboy Country."

He paused to let his words sink in, and was relieved when he saw his aunt's demeanor soften.

"That's true," said Jeanne Marie. "I was impressed with Caitlyn's warmth and openness. She seems genuine. I think she will be willing to consider our opinions and suggestions."

"Exactly," Brodie said. "The harsh reality is Cowboy Country is a done deal. The county zoning board approved it, and the park is going to open whether you like it or not. Isn't it nice to know someone like Caitlyn Moore could be an ally?"

His mother stiffened.

As if her triplet sensed her discomfort, Jeanne Marie put a gentle hand on her sister's arm.

"He's right," Jeanne Marie said. "There's a lot of things I don't like about big business moving into Horseback Hollow. Those of us who oppose it are afraid it will change life as we know it. I've lived here all my life, and my hometown has always been my safe haven. It scares the ever-living daylights out of me to think that I might lose my sanctuary. And I know I speak for the majority of those who have opposed this park.

However, I suppose it's very old-fashioned and maybe even a little backward to think you can freeze a place in time. We fought the good fight to keep Moore Entertainment from moving in, but we lost. Amber is looking forward to being in the Wild West Show. We need to support her. Don't you think it's time that we look for proactive ways to coexist with them?"

"You're family, Brodie. I trust that you would not advocate for a business that didn't have our best interest at heart. I believe in you, and I believe you would never do anything to harm your family."

Now it was his turn to feel as if he'd been slapped, but it wasn't an angry, nasty blow. It was the strangest feeling. She believed in him. She trusted him. The weight and responsibility of the emotions that she had invested in him were heavy.

In his mind, as he backed away from the public spin he had just exercised on his aunt, he was left with a sinking feeling. For the first time in all the years that he had been in business, he really had to examine what he was promising. Because this time when he finished the job and moved on to the next assignment, his work would have lasting effects on the people he...cared about.

He felt like a fraud sitting there—and he wondered if his aunt might be subtly calling his bluff—because he knew he could go into Cowboy Country and make their persona look pretty, but Alden Moore was a businessman. All that good-neighbor hoo-ha amounted to a bunch of smoke and mirrors. Moore hadn't succeeded with his theme park empire by playing nice. Like any businessman worth his salt, he was all about the bottom line and what best benefited Moore Entertainment.

When he'd taken this job, he hadn't realized exactly how close to home the cyclone created by his spin would hit.

He had to do what he had to do. It was his motto. But this time it chafed.

"Besides," Jeanne Marie continued. She was smiling at her sister now. It was that look that Brodie had come to realize meant she was up to something. "There seems to be a charge in the atmosphere when Brodie and Caitlyn are together. I was watching you two at the art festival last weekend. He may claim they're simply platonic, but watch them together once she gets here. You'll see what I mean."

The barbecue took place in the spacious backyard of Jeanne Marie and Deke's home. It was a lovely space, behind the house, separate from the large area where the stage and barn were located for the wedding and reception.

While the barn had been newly renovated for the wedding, this part of the property radiated a lived-in family love. Strands of globe lights illuminated the generous patio area, casting a warm glow over twin trestle tables that seated twenty-six people each. Both tables were full, loaded with food, friends and family—brothers and sisters and nieces and nephews.

This shindig was a fraction of the size of the wedding she'd attended in February—and much more personal. She met Brodie's cousins, Jeanne Marie and Deke's children Stacey and her husband, rancher Colton Foster; Jude and his wife, Gabriella Mendoza; Liam and Julia, who worked at the Hollows Cantina; and Christopher and Kinsley, who worked for the Fortune Foundation. They were the couples who had gotten married at the wedding in February. It was also good to see Amber Rogers, who worked for Cowboy Country and was engaged to Brodie's half brother Jensen.

There were so many Fortunes, it was difficult to keep track of everyone.

She was both relieved and a little terrified when Jeanne Marie directed her and Brodie to sit across from each other at the table, at the same end as Josephine, Deke and herself.

This feast looked like something out of a magazine —one that exemplified family living at its best. There were barbecued ribs and sliced brisket, fresh corn on the cob, green beans, sliced tomatoes, fresh potato salad, coleslaw, baked beans and cornbread. And that was all Caitlyn could fit on her plate. There were other dishes, too, but she didn't want to look like a glutton. She was nervous enough as it was.

When she'd arrived and parked her car in front of the house amidst at least twenty other vehicles, it occurred to her that she wasn't completely sure she was walking into friendly territory. It was common knowledge that the Fortunes were opposed to Cowboy Country. Yet, here she was, accepting the invitation to their family dinner. For all she knew, she might be walking into the angry mob with its torches and pitchforks. But her gut told her that probably wasn't the case. Jeanne Marie seemed levelheaded. Actually, she seemed lovely. And Brodie was family.

She and Brodie worked together. Business was business, but family was sacred.

So this seemed more personal.

Still, she knew she'd be kidding herself to believe that her invitation didn't stem from a little bit of curiosity on their part. The Fortunes had proven that they could be civil when they had invited her parents to the wedding. A family wedding seemed like a much bigger deal than a dinner.

The wedding.

Her stomach flip-flopped at the memory of it. This was the place where it all began.

And, if she was perfectly honest with herself, the place where both she and Brodie had intended for it to end. What happened under the stars stayed under the stars.

She would be doing herself a big favor to remember that once he was done with this project and they had successfully opened the park, he would be on his way back to London or wherever his next conquest led him. Caitlyn's heart tightened at the thought, but she dismissed it.

Tonight's visit was a means to an end—to help Cowboy Country get off on a more secure footing; to get the job done. She was ready and willing to be questioned. Checking her posture, she walked up to the door and took the plunge.

After the whirlwind of introductions, here she sat enjoying the most delicious barbecued brisket she'd ever tasted in her life. She waited for one of the Fortunes to turn the talk to Cowboy Country.

It happened as soon as there was a lull in conversation.

"I was sorry to hear that your daddy had a heart attack," said Jeanne Marie. "How is he doing?"

Caitlyn set down her fork and wiped the corners of her mouth with her napkin. "Thank you for asking. The surgery went well, and he is on the road to recovery. It takes a long time to heal after open-heart surgery."

Everyone at her end of the table nodded solemnly.

"What does that mean for the opening of Cowboy Country?" Deke asked. "Will you push it back?"

Okay. There it is. Here we go.

She glanced at Brodie, who must've taken it as his assignment to answer the question.

"We will absolutely open the park on time," he said unapologetically. There was a little bit of an edge to his voice.

Caitlyn was afraid they might mistake his stance for hostility—or a challenge.

"I'm not sure how well you know my father, but he has several roller-coaster-based theme parks throughout the United States. While he loves his roller coasters, this park is special to him. It's personal. He's always been a big John Wayne fan and a cowboy at heart. Cowboy Country is a bucket list item for him. He almost died when he had that heart attack, and I want to make sure that he sees his dream come true."

The elder Fortunes exchanged glances.

"If you'd rather not talk about this at the dinner

table," Caitlyn said, "I completely understand. However, if you don't mind, I would love to know if you have any questions about the park or if you wouldn't mind sharing what it is that you're opposed to."

For a moment the group at their end of the table didn't say anything. Caitlyn held her breath as she listened to the buzz of cicadas and the murmur of other conversation going on around them. The rest of the dinner party was blissfully oblivious to the serious turn of their conversation.

Deke cleared his throat and sat forward in his chair, but Jeanne Marie placed a gentle hand on his and said, "Horseback Hollow is my family's home. It's the only home I've ever known. It's a safe place where just about everyone knows everyone else. I suppose objections around town have stemmed from fear, from people not wanting Horseback Hollow to change or to be swallowed up by a large conglomerate."

Okay, it was out on the table.

"We understand and respect your concerns," Brodie said. "All I'm asking is that you keep an open mind to the good Moore Entertainment and Cowboy Country can bring to Horseback Hollow. Think about the economic upturn, the money that it stands to pump into the local economy. This really is a win-win situation."

"Moore Entertainment has prided itself on giving back to the community. We host school programs, scholarships and family-friendly work-sharing opportunities. As a matter of fact, for the past several years, Moore Entertainment has been named on *Forbes Magazine*'s top twenty-five family-friendly list for work and life balance. We really do pride ourselves on being good neighbors in the community. And Cowboy Country could be my father's reason to live."

Caitlyn clamped her lips shut. She hadn't meant to say that last part out loud, even if it was the truth. It wasn't a very businesslike thing to say. She was opening her mouth to apologize when the looks on the Fortunes' faces registered. She saw something new.

Empathy and understanding.

If it took everything she had she would make sure Moore Entertainment held up its end of the bargain. Cowboy Country *would* be a good neighbor.

Jeanne Marie nodded, and Caitlyn understood that this part of the conversation was over.

"Could I tempt you with another piece of cornbread, Caitlyn?" She smiled, and Caitlyn smiled back.

"Yes, please. It's delicious."

"Be sure you save some room for dessert," said Josephine. "My sister makes the best red-velvet cake you've ever tasted. I have put on nearly ten pounds since I moved here."

She was so grateful for the life her parents had given her. She'd never wanted for anything—except for a sibling or five, like Brodie had.

And cousins? He had so many cousins she couldn't keep track. No wonder the wedding's guest list had been so long. Inviting the family would've made for a lively, full house, but then when you included everyone in the community and you managed to make room for your adversaries...

Adversaries. It was such an ugly word. Caitlyn was so happy the Fortunes and the Moores were on the road to being allies, but if she had anything to do with it, they would call each other friends. Because tonight, the only torches burning were the ones that lined the patio's perimeter.

Now that dinner was done, Caitlyn was surprised by how little conversation there had been about Moore Entertainment and Cowboy Country. In fact, all that had come up was that Brodie and Caitlyn were working together to open the park. There had been no gasps or digs or declarations about how unwelcome Moore Entertainment and its associates were.

Instead, this big, boisterous Texas family had so much to say about everything else that each one had a hard time getting a word in edgewise. They laughed and talked over each other and enjoyed the meal and each other's company in a way that made Caitlyn feel humbled to be a guest at their table.

Now, as she was helping clear the table, she kept stealing glances at Brodie, who was standing across the patio talking to his brother Oliver and his wife, Shannon. Brodie's gaze snared hers, and he smiled at her from across the way.

There it was again, that attraction that was so powerful it threatened to consume her. Her heart hammered against her breastbone as she smiled back.

"You two are adorable." The voice caught her by surprise, and she accidentally knocked over a glass of water as she whirled around to see who was talking to her. It was Amelia Fortune Chesterfield Drummond. Brodie's sister.

"If you don't mind me saying as much, the two of you could be exceptionally good for each other."

Caitlyn felt heat blossom from the neckline of her scoop-neck dress and climb its way up her neck to her cheeks.

Caitlyn chuckled. "Your brother and I are just friends. And work associates. Really, that's all we are."

Protesting too much, Caitlyn?

She ducked her head as she grabbed a napkin off the table to mop up the spilled water.

"If you say so," Amelia said, not sounding the least bit convinced. "I say just give it time. I know he's not easy to deal with sometimes. He puts up such a hard exterior, but please believe me—deep down he has a heart of gold."

Obviously, it hadn't been Amelia who had convinced him he didn't have a heart.

She seemed to have a pretty good read on her brother.

"He's just been through some…*stuff* in his life," she said. "Circumstances have made him that way."

And she seemed to think she had a pretty good read on Brodie and her as a couple. Caitlyn's heart turned over at the thought. Drawing in a quick breath, she straightened and followed Amelia's gaze to where Brodie was laughing with Oliver and Shannon. It was the most relaxed she'd ever seen him.

What had happened to that beautiful man to make him wear such heavy emotional armor? Was it a woman?

Had he given his heart to someone who treated it so carelessly that he'd closed himself off?

Caitlyn knew how that felt. She'd almost married the guy.

But what was worse, she realized as she stood there feeling alive for the first time in what seemed like years, not only had she allowed the guy to crush her heart, she had allowed him to sweep away all the broken bits and pieces, too. For the longest time, she'd been left with only an empty hole. But Eric had missed some of the pieces, and slowly, they were beginning to grow back together and fill that spot in which she thought she'd never feel again.

If a woman had hurt Brodie, she hoped he wouldn't allow her to continue to rob him of one of life's best pleasures…falling in love.

Amelia knew what had happened to him. And it took every ounce of strength Caitlyn possessed to keep from asking her for details. Because if she did, Amelia would know she'd hit upon something. That Caitlyn and Brodie *could* be good together. Caitlyn had already experienced that live in person, that very first night, before names were exchanged and they knew they'd play a much bigger role in each other's lives.

Brodie glanced her way again, and the smoldering flame she saw in his eyes—as if Amelia weren't standing right there taking it all in—startled her and stoked a gently growing fire deep inside her.

"I hope you'll be patient with him, because I can see that the two of you have a very strong connection."

Amelia must have sensed that Caitlyn didn't know

what to say. After all, what does one say when her head knows good and well she should keep things all business, but her heart and other more vulnerable parts of her body are aching for something completely different—things that should be completely taboo?

"It was the same way with my husband, Quinn. I can assure you, a love like that is worth the time and patience."

Amelia's words made Caitlyn's senses spin. To steady herself, she began stacking plates on the tray.

"You are our guest tonight. You shouldn't be clearing dishes. Go enjoy yourself, please."

Amelia gave an anything but settled glance in Brodie's direction. In fact, it was almost a nod.

"After enjoying that delicious dinner, I can't leave all the work to someone else," said Caitlyn. "I insist on helping."

"Well, in that case, I'll help, too." Amelia laughed. "Otherwise you're going to make me look bad."

As the two of them headed toward the kitchen, Caitlyn wondered if Amelia had any idea of the ringing impact her words had made.

"Married life does seem to be agreeing with you," Brodie said to Oliver and Shannon.

The couple looked at each other with such adoration he had to look away. He glanced over at the table where Caitlyn had been talking to Amelia.

They weren't there anymore.

His gaze combed the area, and he glimpsed the two of them as they disappeared inside the back door that led to the kitchen, each of them holding a tray loaded with dishes. Brodie took a step in that direction as the door banged shut behind them. He wished he would've noticed sooner, and he would've been there to help.

"We've never been happier," Oliver said. "I highly recommend it."

"Caitlyn is so nice." Shannon hitched little Ollie up on her hip.

"Yes, she is," he said. He knew what she meant, and he knew he should clarify that they were strictly platonic—or at least they were now.

His cousin, Galen Fortune Jones, must've overheard Oliver and Shannon's less than subtle verbal nudging.

"She may be nice, but some men just aren't cut out for the husband thing."

Oliver and Shannon made protesting noises.

"Those men obviously haven't met the right women," said Shannon. "Or they are not attracted to women. But hey, I'm not judging. I'm all for live and let live."

Galen frowned. "Believe me, I am attracted to women. That's exactly my point. I'm attracted to *women*. Lots of women. I see no reason to limit myself to just one. And I know Brodie feels the same way. Hence the Enduring Bachelorhood Club of Horseback Hollow. Welcome to the club, cousin."

Galen guffawed and held out his fist for a bump. Brodie complied, but his heart wasn't really in it.

There was a time when he might've been president of an Enduring Bachelorhood Club, but tonight it seemed like the last place he wanted to be. It just seemed…sad.

Someone put some music on, and several people

started dancing. Oliver took Shannon's hand and pulled her a few steps away from Brodie and Galen.

"We will leave you two enduring bachelors alone," he said. "My wife and I have better things to do."

He pulled Shannon into his arms, and the two of them began swaying to the music, lost in their own little world.

He wasn't really in the mood to stay and discuss enduring bachelorhood with his cousin. "I'm going to go into the kitchen and get something to drink. May I bring you something?"

Galen held up the beer in his hand. "Nah, I'm good, thanks. I'll catch you later, bro."

In the kitchen, Caitlyn was helping Amelia scoop leftovers into plastic containers. His mother was washing dishes, and Jeanne Marie was drying them.

The buzz of conversation—something about the secret ingredient in Jeanne Marie's red-velvet-cake recipe—stopped when he entered the room.

"I suppose the ingredient is not a secret any longer if you tell everyone," he said.

"Look who's come to help us," said his mother.

"I have a feeling he didn't come in here to help us," said Amelia, a knowing smile spreading across her face.

"She's right," said Brodie. "I've come to rescue Caitlyn from a life of servitude."

"Run," said Amelia, taking the serving spoon out of Caitlyn's hand. "Run while you can. Save yourself."

"Absolutely," said Jeanne Marie. She shook her head. "Where are my manners? I was so enjoying talking to you that I kept you in the kitchen far too long. You two run along and have some fun. Go on now. Skedaddle."

"It was such a lovely meal," Caitlyn said. "I hate to leave you with the mess."

"We won't hear of it," said Josephine. "You've already done more than your share. More than I can say for some people."

She arched a brow at Brodie.

"We'll go find Galen and send him right in," said Brodie. "I understand he's looking for something to do."

In a stage whisper he said to Caitlyn, "We'd better make a run for it while we can."

He offered her his arm, and she took it, a strange smile on her face.

Once they were back outside, a slow country song came on.

"Dance with me?"

He didn't give her a chance to refuse. He simply wrapped his arms around her, and they joined the others who had turned the patio into an after-dinner dance floor and began swaying to the music.

"Your family is wonderful," she whispered. "Not nearly as scary as I thought they'd be."

"You're brave," he said, inhaling deeply as she leaned in close. Her scent and the feel of her in his arms took him back to that first night. His body responded and the base, most primal part of him wanted to ask her if she wanted to take a stroll down meteor lane. But there wasn't a meteor shower tonight, and holding her like this felt more intimate than taking her back to the field by the pond and peeling off her denim jacket and that sexy green sundress and claiming the prize underneath. "Most of the time they still scare me."

Not that he didn't want to claim that prize.

Holding her like this felt like ten giant leaps forward. Especially when she looked up at him. For a moment he could've sworn he glimpsed forever in her eyes. He pulled her closer so that it wouldn't slip away.

All he had to do was lower his head a few inches, and his lips would be on hers, but she said, "I need to go. Will you walk me to my car?"

The distance and perspective he gained while she was getting her handbag and saying thank-you and good-night to his family was a godsend.

He'd almost kissed her. Right there on the patio in front of anyone who might've been paying attention, which was probably more people than would've owned up to it.

He'd gotten lost in the moment. Lost in a wonderful evening where she had been magnificent with his family. She'd won them over with her grace and ease.

This wasn't a personal victory; this was about getting the job done. It was a victory for Cowboy Country. Now that they were on the right track, he needed to keep his mind on the job and his hands off his boss's daughter.

As he walked Caitlyn to her car, she must've sensed the shift in him.

"Why does intimacy scare you, Brodie?"

"Intimacy doesn't scare me." He crossed his arms.

"What happened to you to make you put up such a wall?"

Nobody had ever asked him the question. He knew

the answer, but he couldn't talk about it. Because that would mean he'd have to return to dark, emotional places he swore he'd never visit again.

"What's in the past can't be changed," he said. "There's no sense in rehashing it."

She opened her car door and slid behind the wheel.

"Sometimes the only way to exorcise your demons is to face them."

"They're not demons unless you allow them to get the best of you."

She shook her head, and there was so much pity in her eyes, he had to look away.

"Suit yourself," she said as she started the car.

What could he say to that?

Nothing.

Instead, he opted for watching the taillights of Caitlyn's car grow dimmer as she drove away.

Chapter Seven

All week long Brodie had been furious with himself. What the bloody hell was the matter with him?

At the barbecue Friday night, he'd gotten swept up in the moment.

All weekend long he had tried to tell himself he'd simply been jazzed because Caitlyn had won over his family so easily and naturally. But a nagging little bugger of a voice deep inside kept insisting that was wrong. That he wasn't being honest with himself. That he was terminally attracted to Caitlyn Moore.

Brodie tried to remind himself of his A-number-one rule: *do not sleep with the clients.* Now amended to include: *do not kiss the clients.*

Before, that had always been a given, along with *do not mix business with pleasure.*

He would've been wise to have talked Caitlyn out of attending the barbecue, but he usually didn't associate family gatherings with pleasure. This woman had a way of inserting herself into places in his life that made him...uncomfortable. And now she was asking questions—personal questions. Questions about what made him tick, what made him so damn defensive.

Personal relationships made him defensive. If she was so bloody intuitive, why couldn't she figure that out without grilling him?

What was it about Caitlyn Moore that had his self-control puddling in a pool at his feet?

And then, even against his best judgment, he found himself stepping over that pool like a madman, possessed with the need to get closer to her.

Brodie simply wasn't cut out to fall in love. And Caitlyn...she was so family-oriented.

This had the potential to be one hell of a bloody mess, didn't it?

Granted, she was a beautiful woman, but he'd worked with plenty of pretty women before, and he'd never had this much trouble keeping his mind on the job.

It was just about sex. Nothing more. It was some crazy chemical reaction—what did they call it? Pheromones? Whatever it was, it was making him lose control. And there was nothing Brodie Fortune Hayes loathed more than being out of control.

Logic told him the sooner he could get back to London, the better off everyone would be. But the part of his brain that was still working reminded him that his contract dictated that he still had more than two weeks here in Horseback Hollow.

Really, if he thought about it—and kept his mind on the job—it wasn't a lot of time to get done what he needed to do to get this park up and running to Alden Moore's satisfaction and secure the recommendation for the Tokyo project.

It really was quite simple. He needed to quit thinking about Caitlyn in any terms other than business. Because doing that was making things harder on him than the job needed to be.

In that vein, this morning he had gotten up extra early—well, if truth be told he hadn't been able to sleep—and got into the office early enough to avoid Monday-morning office coffee chat. He'd brought in his own coffee in his stainless-steel travel mug. It was his own brew from his French press, and it was head and shoulders over the dirty dishwater from the coffee machine in the break room. It would also buy him a little more time and give him that extra caffeinated edge he needed to see Caitlyn this morning.

He wasn't kidding himself; he wasn't pretending he could avoid her all day. He would have to see her eventually. Avoiding her would be unprofessional and downright juvenile.

That's what he was thinking when Caitlyn burst into his office, all smiles and electric energy.

"I've finally figured out how to fix the park," she said, those green eyes so bright and lovely it hurt him to look at them.

"You figured it out?" His voice sounded as exhausted as he felt. "Please enlighten me."

"Yes, I have. What's wrong with you? You're scowling."

He sat back in his chair. "Nothing's wrong with me, thank you. I was in the middle of something, and you interrupted."

She frowned at him. "I'm sorry. Should I come back later? Although really, this can't wait."

He crossed his arms and put his palms in the air. "I'm waiting."

He wasn't sure if she rolled her eyes at him or simply shrugged off his sarcasm—probably both—but it was obvious she was not allowing him to bring her down.

"What Cowboy Country needs is the perspective of genuine cowboys. It needs the heart of folks like the Fortunes—your family. And we need to draft a solid plan of how we intend to give back to the community. Once that's done, I want to present it to the community at the next town hall meeting. If we can get on the meeting agenda, we can have an open forum and encourage an exchange with the citizens of Horseback Hollow. I want your mother and aunt to use their influence to get us on the agenda. I almost called you this weekend to tell you about this, but I didn't. Maybe I should have, because obviously you didn't have a very good weekend."

Maybe she should have? Did she realize what she was suggesting?

No. Because she probably wasn't suggesting what he had in mind. The thought took his dark mood down another notch.

He dragged his hands down his face, trying to scrub some of the bad out of his mood. How could she be so chipper on a Monday morning? On *this* Monday morning, after *that* Friday night?

Obviously, she hadn't taken the dance or the near-miss kiss to heart the way he had.

That was sobering.

And a little bit liberating.

"I'm sorry," he said. "I had a rough night. I didn't sleep very well."

She studied him for a moment, and he would've given his BMW if he could've known what she was thinking.

"Everything okay?" Her expression changed from upbeat to concern. "Your family didn't change their mind about Cowboy Country, did they? I thought everything went so well."

"No. No worries. My family loves you. How about we start over? Or at least let me start with talking to Jeanne Marie about getting us on the next town-meeting agenda. If we do get to address the citizens, it will put us one step closer to recruiting the genuine cowboys. But let's tackle the town meeting first."

Caitlyn was onto something. She could feel it in her bones.

If the Fortunes were willing to come around, then the rest of the town couldn't be too hard to win over. Maybe it was optimism, but Caitlyn was sure that they could do it. Especially after Jeanne Marie had agreed to help them get a place on the town meeting agenda.

She'd also shared a nugget of information that had the potential to be golden: apparently the on-property hotel her father had planned to build—the Cowboy Condos— was one of the biggest sticking points with some of the staunchest adversaries. Jeanne Marie couldn't tell them why, but with a little bit of internal digging, she was able to find the name of an investor who had pulled out of the deal—Hank Harvey, a venture capitalist from Dallas. He was going to be in Lubbock on Wednesday and had agreed to drive to Horseback Hollow to meet Caitlyn and Brodie at the stalled jobsite to talk about what went wrong.

According to Brodie, who had talked to him, Mr. Harvey was prepared to give them an earful.

Caitlyn hated to jump to snap judgments, but Hank Harvey rubbed her the wrong way from the moment he'd opened his mouth. It was eight o'clock in the morning, and his breath reeked of alcohol, and that wasn't even the worst of it.

Strike one: when she introduced herself and offered her hand for him to shake, this textbook Texas good ol' boy raked his gaze down her body as he gave her fingertips a lackluster press.

"Ma'am." Now his gaze veered somewhere over her right shoulder. She wanted to turn around to see who he was looking at. Before she could, he turned and vigorously pumped Brodie's hand with a solid man-grip and slapped him on the back.

"Brodie Fortune Hayes. Good to meet ya, man. Are you kin to *that* bunch of Fortunes?"

"Guilty as charged," Brodie said.

As the *boys* exchanged pleasantries, Caitlyn glanced around the empty construction site. Located on the east side of the property, the parcel was far enough away from the park so it would not interfere with business as usual. The two ventures were separate, but the original intent had been for them to feed each other. Out-of-town guests coming to the park would stay at the hotel, and exhausted revelers, tired out after a long day of Cowboy Country fun—or those wanting to extend their visit— could book a room and stay right on the property.

After the construction had come to a halt, the work-site, which had sat untouched for several weeks, had been secured with chain-link fencing. The leveled ground was mottled by the elements and littered with trash; weeds grew amidst the infrastructure, which the workers had begun to build before the investors had pulled out. The sky was overcast, and it was a little cooler today than it had been recently. The clouds seemed to cast everything around them in gloomy shades of gray. As it stood, this part of the property looked like a razed ghost town.

It was a little sad and eerie.

"So you're from London, are ya now?" Hank asked, hitching the waistband of his blue jeans over his ample belly. "The wife keeps pushing for me to take her there, but Vegas is more my style. No offense to you and your queen and all. I'm tellin' you, if ya know the right people you can get in on some pretty sweet gambling junkets in Vegas. Let me know if you're interested. I can hook ya up."

Okay... Let's stay on topic.

"Mr. Harvey," Caitlyn said. "We really appreciate you meeting us out here today. I know you have a plane to catch in a couple of hours. So we won't keep you long. We are looking into the possibility of resuming construction on the Cowboy Condos. Apparently, there was a problem that caused you and the other investors to withdraw support? Brodie and I are trying to piece together what happened."

Hank pulled his cell phone out of his back pocket and looked at something displayed on the screen. He didn't answer her.

Maybe she needed to be more specific.

"Would you mind telling us the reason you withdrew your support from the project?"

He typed something on his phone with his fat thumbs.

"Uh, yeah. It wasn't a…" he muttered as he typed.

When he looked up—strike two: his gaze landed and stayed on her breasts.

"Uh, yeah. It just wasn't a…" His voice trailed off. "Wasn't a good investment. Didn't work for me."

Caitlyn crossed her arms over her chest, shielding herself from his invasion of privacy. Brodie must've noticed, because he stepped slightly in front of her and diverted the creep's attention.

"What didn't work for you, exactly?" he asked.

"All kinds of things," Hank murmured. "So now, do you actually live in London? I hear it's one of the most expensive cities in the world."

"Yes, I own a flat in Notting Hill. Mr. Harvey, would

you mind being more specific? Why did the project not work for you? What about it caused you to pull your investment? We need to know so that we can make corrections going forward."

"Hank. Please call me Hank. Mr. Harvey is my dad. I'm Hank."

"Fair enough. Hank it is." Caitlyn could see Brodie's profile. He smiled at Hank's nonsense.

Caitlyn wanted to stomp on Harvey's toe. Why was he being so chummy with Brodie when he was having a difficult time answering her questions with complete sentences?

Then came the coup de grâce.

Strike three: misogynistic creep not only turned his back on her, he actually clapped Brodie on the back and motioned with his fat head for Brodie to walk with him.

And Brodie did. Giving him the benefit of the doubt, he cast a remorseful glance back at Caitlyn. From that glance she read, *Bear with me. This might be the only way to get the info out of the guy.*

Caitlyn should've stomped his foot when she'd had the chance.

"Shoddy construction?" Caitlyn asked once she and Brodie were back in the office. "What the heck is that supposed to mean?"

Brodie could tell she was irritated. Personally, he'd wanted to deck the guy when he'd noticed him ogling Caitlyn.

"That's what he said. I'm sorry. Don't shoot the messenger. He said he didn't want his name associated with an inferior product. When Cisco Mendoza withdrew from the project, Harvey said he was done."

She stammered a bit. "Inferior product? How— What was inferior?"

Cisco Mendoza was engaged to his cousin, Jeanne Marie's youngest daughter Delaney Fortune Jones, but Brodie hadn't had the opportunity to get to know him since Cisco had only been in town almost as short a time as Brodie had. From what he understood, Mendoza had been a real-estate developer in Miami, who had been handpicked to head up Cowboy Country's hotel division—to act as a rainmaker of sorts and bring in investors. From where Brodie sat, it seemed Mendoza had done more damage than good. That's one of the reasons Brodie hadn't been keen on talking to him about Cowboy Country. Brodie needed Alden Moore as a client. He wanted to come in and assess the situation with fresh eyes and not be influenced by someone who had left with a bad taste in his mouth.

Apparently, after Cisco left, operations at the park had gone from bad to worse. Shortly after that, his supervisor—a man named Kent Stephens—had thrown in the towel, and then Alden Moore had suffered the heart attack.

It was too soon to pump Alden for more information. It was a sore subject, and Brodie didn't want to bring him any stress. He had been hired to fix things, not tally up the problems and present them to Moore.

In fact, wouldn't it be nice if, in addition to opening the park, he could sort out the issues with the Cowboy Condos and present Alden with a new workable plan?

"I'll talk to Cisco and ask him to level with us," Brodie said.

Caitlyn nodded. "Yes, please. There has to be more to the story than what Harvey Wallbanger is telling us."

Brodie snorted at the name.

The color spiked in Caitlyn's cheeks.

"Not only did the jerk completely marginalize me, but if what he's saying is true, I'm really worried about my father. Brodie, why would a man who has built his name in the theme-park industry settle for something of bad quality? It just doesn't make sense."

Brodie had wondered the same thing himself.

"And did you see him staring at my—" She gestured toward her bodice. "He wouldn't even look me in the eye."

Brodie cleared his throat. "Well, I wasn't going to say anything, but since you brought it up, yes, I did notice, and I wanted to punch the guy."

Her face went soft, and her lips curved up at the corners. "You would've done that for me? Defended my honor?"

He nodded.

"But you do realize I hate violence. So you did the right thing by distracting him instead."

They sat there in silence for a moment. Brodie stared at his clenched fist and then flexed his fingers because she'd just said she didn't like violence. He didn't, either. Yet he'd been perfectly prepared to defend her.

"At least the guy left us with some information to go on," Caitlyn said.

Brodie looked up and fixed his gaze on hers. He

didn't find it difficult to look at those beautiful eyes. They were actually quite mesmerizing.

Through the hazy fog that was addling his brain, he heard himself saying, "Don't worry. I'll talk with Cisco and find out the rest of the story. We'll find a way to make this right."

Chapter Eight

A knock on the frame of her open office door made Caitlyn look up from her computer. When she saw Brodie standing there, her stomach did a low flip that made her breath catch.

"Hi," she said, noticing the rolled-up papers he held. They looked like blueprints.

"Hi, do you have a minute?" He smiled. "I have good news."

She motioned him in. "I'd give you an entire day for some good news. Please, do tell."

"Let's go over here where I can roll out these." With the blueprints, he gestured toward a small conference table set up on the far side of the rectangular room.

"Are these what I hope they are?" she asked.

"If you mean the plans for the Cowboy Condos,

you're spot on." She watched as he began spreading them out on the table.

"Where did you get them?" she asked.

"I made a couple of calls late yesterday and got in touch with Cisco Mendoza. He dropped them off and filled in some of the missing pieces."

She narrowed her eyes and cocked her head. "You met with Mendoza without me?"

Brodie held up his hand. "I did, but don't get upset. He left for business in Red Rock this morning. He's training for his new job with the Fortune Foundation. If I hadn't gotten together with him last night, he wouldn't have been available until next week."

"You should've called me."

"Really? You wanted me to call you after hours?"

Yes, I wish you would.

She could've read so much into his gaze, his tone, that question. Instead, she put her hands in her lap and squeezed them together so tightly that her nails dug into her skin. That touchstone brought her back to her senses.

"Of course, you can always call me…"

But she let the words hang there so he could form his own conclusion.

"Next time I will."

He smiled at her, and there was that instant rush attraction that pulled her right in. She could've sworn he felt it, too.

She smiled and looked away. "I'm surprised Mendoza was willing to meet with you on such short notice. Because from what I understand, he didn't leave here a very happy man."

"Obviously, you don't know that Cisco is engaged to my cousin Delaney," he said.

Caitlyn laughed. "Why am I not surprised? Is anyone in this town not related to the Fortunes?"

Brodie considered the question. "Not many people."

"Wait," Caitlyn said. "Cisco and Delaney were not at the barbecue, were they?"

"No. They were in Miami packing up Cisco's apartment. He's moving to Horseback Hollow permanently. They just got back, and Cisco left for Red Rock this morning. That's why last night's meeting was more like a hand-off of the blueprints than an actual meeting. He brought me the blueprints and told me his side of the story. Really, there wasn't much to tell."

Caitlyn blinked at him, reality eclipsing the attraction she'd felt just seconds ago.

"I thought you said you had good news."

"Sometimes good news comes in small packages. Mendoza didn't have much to say, but what he said was important. He didn't back out because of shoddy construction. It had nothing to do with the quality of the hotel. It was the style that had everyone in an uproar. Apparently, the architect your father hired had designed something very kitschy—buildings shaped like cowboy hats with cowboy-boot-shaped windows, that sort of thing."

Brodie raised his eyebrows for emphasis, and Caitlyn cringed.

"That sounds dreadful."

She crossed her arms and thought about it for a moment.

"However, I hate to admit that my dad may have

gotten a little bit carried away. You have no idea how this cowboy obsession of his can take over his better judgment. Never in a business sense, but sometimes the kitschy-tacky knows no bounds."

Brodie laughed. "Well, it's good to know that even the master can get it wrong once or twice."

"Yeah, he'd never admit that. I'm sure he would give his eyeteeth to stay in a cowboy-hat-shaped hotel."

Looking past Brodie's good humor, she saw true reverence in his eyes. He really did respect her dad. For some reason she found it a little curious given his tendency to keep his own family at arm's length.

She remembered what Amelia had said and had the urge to ask him about it. But he changed the subject, and the moment was lost.

"Apparently, Cisco Mendoza left because of creative differences. He knew one of the main reasons the locals were opposed to the park was because of the kitsch factor. He'd had a whole new set of plans drawn up, but his supervisor, Kent Stephens, refused to take the plans to the next level. Mendoza seems to believe that Stephens was in bed with the original architect, and that's why he put up roadblocks to keep Mendoza's plans from your father. The investors left when Mendoza pulled out. Stephens left about a week later, and then that's when things happened with your father."

"It all makes sense," Caitlyn said. "You said he had the plans drawn up?"

Brodie nodded.

"Did he happen to mention the name of the architect?" she asked.

"He did one better."

Brodie lifted the cowboy hat blueprints to reveal another set underneath.

"Take a look at this. This design is much earthier, a better complement to the feel of Horseback Hollow. Cisco ran it by some of the locals, and they were much more amenable to something like this that better fit into the landscape. In fact, if landscaped properly, it would probably almost disappear rather than sitting out like a dozen giant cowboy hats that somebody forgot to put away."

"This makes me so happy," she said. "Having the blueprints already drawn up and basically endorsed by the town puts us so much further ahead than I ever dreamed possible at this point."

"Glad I could help," he said.

They were standing so close to each other *looking at the blueprint* that their arms were touching. She stood there for a moment reveling in the nearness of him. She knew this was dangerous; she knew pushing this defied all logic.

Yet she moved just a fraction of an inch closer so she could feel the heat of him against her.

"I think we need to celebrate," she said.

If she turned just so to her left and he did the same, they'd be standing face-to-face, close enough for their lips to touch, for their bodies to be flush.

"I vote for that." His voice was deep and raspy, the sound sweet as syrup. "What did you have in mind?"

She knew what she had in mind, and she was fairly certain it was exactly what he had in mind, too.

Her desk phone rang, ruining the moment.

"Are you going to get that?" he asked.

Of course she was.

She moved away from him and felt an almost palpable change of altitude.

"Yes, Janie," she said, trying not to sound annoyed with this woman, who was only doing her job.

"Les Campbell is on the line. May I put him through?"

"Yes, please."

Please don't let this be bad news.

Seconds later, Les said, "Hello, Ms. Moore. The Twin Rattlers coaster is ready for its inaugural run, and we were wondering if you'd like to take a ride?"

Oh, good!

She glanced at Brodie, who had his back to her, leafing through the pages of the blueprints. She wondered idly if he knew how to read the pages beyond the elevation on the first page.

He was a man of so many talents…her gaze followed the line of his broad shoulders. He was wearing a white dress shirt tucked into trousers that did a fine job showcasing his…assets.

Caitlyn tore her gaze away. She was as bad as Hank Harvey.

No, she wasn't. This was different.

Completely different.

"I'd love to, Les. Thanks so much for thinking of me. Oh, and Les, there will be two of us. We will see you in fifteen minutes."

"Sounds good, ma'am."

She wished people would stop calling her *ma'am*.

It made her feel old. But she supposed it was a sign of respect. Besides, Les was one of the nicer members of the crew, and she appreciated how hard he worked and the way he went out of his way to be nice—not just to her, but to others, too.

She hung up the phone.

"Come on," she said to Brodie. "Let's go. I know how we're going to celebrate."

He turned around and arched a brow at her. A dimple winked at her from his cheeks. "And what exactly are we going to do?"

"We're going to ride a roller coaster."

His smile faded, replaced by a *you've got to be kidding me* look.

"Um. No, thank you. You go ahead, though."

"Brodie, it's the inaugural ride of the Twin Rattler. This is the big-ticket ride. The moneymaker that's going to draw in people from all over the country. It's an honor to do the inaugural ride."

His brow knit. "Even better reason to say no. I'd rather not be the rattlers' guinea pig. Sounds like a likely chance of being eaten. Or flung into the next town."

She cocked her head and looked at him. "Are you afraid?"

Brodie shrugged but then shook his head. "No, I'm not afraid. I simply have common sense. That's all."

"You're a chicken."

"You're a bully."

They both burst out laughing.

"What are we? Twelve years old?" she said.

"Apparently so. I never knew you were a mean girl, Caitlyn Moore."

"I'm not. I swear. You don't have to do anything you don't want to do. But I'm not a big chicken. I'm going to ride the Twin Rattlers."

"So you're that confident that this ride is ready to go?"

"Yes, I am. My father is the roller-coaster king. To date, no one has ever died on a single ride in a single one of his theme parks. He handpicked the rides for Cowboy Country, and I highly doubt that he would want to end such a stellar no-injury record at his bucket list park. I have to trust that everything will be fine."

He looked at her for a moment, a look that seemed to reach all the way into her soul.

"You really do see the best in everyone, don't you?"

She shrugged. "I try. There's good in everyone. Sometimes you just have to look past the roadblocks that they throw in your way."

He nodded, and she took it as a nonverbal signal that he knew exactly what…or who…she was talking about.

"With that endorsement, how can I say no? Besides, I don't want to listen to you calling me a chicken, you insufferable bully. But before we go, let me make a phone call. This is a photo op, exactly the kind of fun, positive story we should be getting out there into the community."

Truvy Jennings from the county newspaper, *The Cross Town Crier*, said she would send someone out in fifteen minutes and with that, Caitlyn and Brodie made their way to the Twin Rattlers, which was the park's crowning glory, situated in the very center of the property.

When they got there, Caitlyn was surprised that Les Campbell and his team were the only other people there.

"Where is everyone?" Caitlyn asked.

Les gestured to Caitlyn and Brodie. "Right here. You're all present and accounted for."

"But Les, usually when we do the first run, there's enough people to fill the entire train."

"I'm sorry, ma'am," he said. "We wanted to make this run special for you. We thought you'd like to do this by yourself."

By herself? No, this was about team building.

Les frowned. "I suppose we could delay it for a couple of hours so we could round up others."

"A representative of the newspaper will be here shortly," Brodie interjected. "We need to do this now. A delay might make people think we're having problems."

He glanced at his watch and shifted uncomfortably. There was something he wasn't telling her.

"Les, is everything okay?"

"Ma'am…um…may I speak candidly with you?"

"Of course, Les. Always."

He exhaled. "We tried to round up a crowd, but we had a hard time finding people who were interested."

"No one wanted to do the first run?" Brodie's voice had an edge. Caitlyn feared that what was coming next wasn't going to be pretty. But she saw him take a deep breath and steady himself.

"I suppose it was spur of the moment. I think we need to schedule some participation for later in the week. Everyone in the park should be familiar with the rides and the layout of the park."

Les nodded his agreement, but she could see he was stiff and possibly afraid to do or say anything else.

Brodie turned to Caitlyn. "After we're finished here, let's schedule meetings with the department heads and look at the calendar to plan a mandatory pre-opening orientation for all employees. I want this place to be happier than the happiest place in the universe."

Oh, gosh, he needs to have some fun. He needs to loosen up.

Somehow she was going to have to make him see that he needed to take a gentler approach. They'd have to talk about it later because in the distance, Caitlyn spotted Truvy Jennings from the paper approaching them with her camera in hand. Apparently, she'd decided to cover the story herself.

Great. Just great.

"Here comes Truvy from the paper. I need you to work your magic and convince her that this unceremonious ride for two is exactly what we'd planned. Can you give her your best impersonation of a roller-coaster-lover?"

"I will bring nothing less." He winked at her, back in PR professional mode.

Watching him as he greeted Truvy and had her melting under his charm, no one would ever know just a moment ago he was ready to dismiss everyone who might refuse to ride a roller coaster. Especially when he hadn't been very eager to ride himself.

Then again, he'd changed his tune once she'd coerced him.

The man was a puzzle who constantly kept her wondering who he really was deep down: Passionate lover? Stern dictator? Emotional stoic? Public charmer?

But once they were seated in the Twin Rattlers' first car, and he reached out and took her hand, her doubt melted away under his touch.

Then the ride took off, carrying them up, up, up the first huge climb. He never let go of her hand as it spilled down the first drop and curved into the first twist.

They laughed and screamed and held their hands up in the air—his fingers protectively laced through hers. The roller coaster definitely brought out Brodie's uninhibited side, and Caitlyn loved it. It was the most fun she'd had in a really long time. But it stopped being fun when the train came to a jerking halt, halfway through the ride atop the highest point.

"Are you kidding me?" Brodie said as he searched Caitlyn's face to see if she could offer an explanation for what was happening. "Is this some sort of joke?"

She shook her head. "If it is, I'm not in on it, I assure you."

Brodie let go of her hand so he could lean forward, to try and see what was going on below, but the height gave him a pit of vertigo, and he sat back.

"Do you have your cell phone with you?" he asked. "Maybe we can call someone and see what's going on."

"I left mine on my desk because I don't have any pockets."

Brodie raked his hand through his hair, trying to tame his mounting frustration. "I tossed mine onto my desk, too, before I came into your office with the blueprints. I should've grabbed it before we left."

"I'm sure it won't take them very long. Les assured me that all the kinks had been worked out."

Brodie threw his hands up in the air. "And we were gullible enough to believe him. No wonder nobody else wanted to go on this inaugural ride. I'll bet Truvy is getting one hell of a story. This is simply not acceptable—"

He stopped midsentence when he realized Caitlyn was frowning at him.

"Well, it's not."

Caitlyn covered her face with both hands. "Can we not do this up here? Please?"

He could hear the tinges of panic in her voice. Her breath was a little shallow.

"Not everything is controllable," she said. "Things happen. Rides break down. People don't always perform the way you expect them to or want them to. Life is messy. You can't control everything."

She was shaking. He took her hand.

"Hey, I'm sorry. It's okay. It's going to be okay. Really."

He slipped his arm around her and pulled her in close. She took a deep breath and settled into him.

It was a beautiful day. Not too hot, with a pleasant breeze every now and again that ruffled the treetops.

"Really, this is the best view in the house."

He felt her relax a little bit more as he rubbed her shoulder. With his free hand, he pointed. "Look over there. That's Main Street. It looks different from up here, doesn't it?"

She nodded, her breathing growing steadier. "It's pretty. I didn't realize there were so many trees."

He traced where Main Street would have continued under the canopy of oaks to a stretch of open highway. "I believe if you follow that highway on down, that's the road that leads to my aunt Jeanne Marie and uncle Deke's ranch."

"Everything looks so much smaller up here. Down on the ground everything seems so much closer together. I never asked this, but where do you live?"

He gestured behind them.

"I live in the complete opposite direction. About five miles from the Fortune ranch. I am renting a carriage house from my brother's father-in-law. Oliver stayed there before he and Shannon were married. I'm lucky to have it since rental property in Horseback Hollow is hard to come by. If not for the Singleton house, I probably might have been forced to bunk with my extended family. Even the thought of that scares me."

Caitlyn gave him a little nudge with her shoulder. "You have a wonderful family. I don't understand why living with them would be such a horrible thing."

He sighed. "There's such a thing as too much togetherness. My family takes a nice thing and turns it into smothering."

"When I was a little girl I used to wish for a large family. Don't get me wrong, I adore my parents. But my dad has always been a workaholic—"

Brodie smiled. "A man after my own heart."

"I've been wanting to thank you for being so good to my father while he's been ill. I mean, I know he's paying you handsomely—as he should—but you seemed to connect better with him than most people—certainly better than my ex. I saw that when you defended me to him the other day. Granted, he's trying to be a little more relaxed because of his condition, but if you hadn't handled that just right it could've turned pretty ugly. I've seen it happen before."

Brodie shrugged. He liked hearing her open up about her family, her childhood and her past.

"Tell me about your ex," he said. "What happened?"

She tried to wave him off. But then she sighed. "Two weeks before the wedding, I found out that he'd slept with someone else. The worst part was that it was someone he just picked up one night. He was willing to sacrifice everything that we had for one night with a stranger."

"So, was that your motivation for sleeping with me after the wedding?"

Oh, hell. Why had he said that? The look in her eyes made him want to kick himself.

Then she lifted her chin. "What if I said yes? Is it only acceptable for men to pick up women?"

"I'm not judging," said Brody. "But you sound like you're the one who isn't comfortable with the idea of one-night stands."

She shrugged and looked away.

He wondered if they would be sitting here like this right now, getting so personal, if not for that one night in February.

Of course they'd both be here at Cowboy Country, and they'd probably be attracted to each other—this thing between them was magnetic—but he'd bet money that they would both be all business. They might wonder, but if he'd known out of the starting gate that she was Alden Moore's daughter, he probably wouldn't have acted.

As far as he was concerned, that one-night stand in February was one of the best things that had ever happened to him.

"When a guy cheats, when *anybody* cheats," Brodie said, "it's not a reflection on the person who was cheated on. It's a reflection of the cheater's cowardice. There's not a thing in the world wrong with you, Cait. This one's all on him."

She turned back to him. "You sound like you speak from experience."

"In a roundabout way. My father cheated on my mother. He treated her terribly."

"Poor Josephine."

Brody nodded. "She didn't deserve it. No one does."

"As far as I know, my dad has never cheated on my mother. He may be a lot of things, but at least he's always been an honorable man. But despite the fact that I'm twenty-nine years old, in my father's eyes I will forever be twelve. Know what I mean?"

"No. Not really. I mean, I understand what you're saying, but I have not personally experienced that. I never really had a relationship with my natural father."

"But your mother is lovely. She seems to dote on you."

"My mother *is* a lovely person. I've just had a very different upbringing than you."

"Tell me about your childhood. I want to hear everything."

She snuggled in closer to him and right about then she could have persuaded him to talk about anything, especially if it meant that he could hold her like this.

She fit so perfectly next to him.

"Really, it's a rather boring story. I went to boarding schools, and then I went off to university. I started my own company, and here I am."

She nudged him again. "I don't want the Brodie Fortune Hayes bio. I want to hear about the real you."

He held up his free hand in a one-shoulder shrug, keeping his other arm snugly around her.

"I'm sort of a what-you-see-is-what-you-get type of guy—"

"No, you're not. You are much more complicated than that, and I want to know what's made you that way."

He stiffened, but he resisted the urge to squirm. Because anyone who knew anything about body language understood that was one of the first signs that a person was uncomfortable.

"You may ask me five questions," he said. "And I will answer them."

"Really?" She glanced up at him. As he nodded, his gaze focused on those lips of hers. They were so full and kissable...and tempting. His body responded.

"Then I get to ask you five."

"It's a deal," she said. "Tell me about your father."

That was one way to kill the mood. How was he supposed to know she'd zero right in where it hurt?

"That's not a question," he said.

"What is this, *Jeopardy*? You didn't specify that it had to be phrased as an interrogative. That one doesn't count. Let me rephrase it. Will you tell me about your father?"

"No. Next question."

"That is so not fair. You didn't answer my first one."

"Yes, I did. You asked if I would tell you about my father. I answered no. Next question."

"I suppose we could sit here in silence until you answer me."

"I forgot to mention that *open season* expires once the ride starts again."

He felt her tense up again. "Oh, right. Thanks for reminding me. For a moment we were having so much fun, I forgot we were stuck."

Brodie sighed. "My parents were divorced when I was three. I never really knew my natural father. My mother remarried Sir Simon John Chesterfield—he's Amelia's natural father."

"Is he also Oliver's father?"

"Is that your second question?"

"What? No! I was just continuing conversation. That doesn't count."

"Just so you can't say I'm not a nice guy, I'll give you that one since we are a complicated bunch. Oliver is older than I am. We have the same natural father. I have four half siblings: Amelia, Jensen, Charles and Lucie."

"That's amazing. Not only do you have this expansive extended family, your immediate family is like an army, too."

"You have no idea. Next question."

He wanted to steer the conversation away from his family before Caitlyn started digging any deeper. That was all she needed to know, anyway. He'd set himself up for this, left himself wide open when he'd given her free rein. He should've set parameters, but the nearness of her made his senses spin, messed with the equilibrium of his common sense.

"Have you ever had your heart broken?" she asked, stealing a glance at him.

He nodded, and she rested her head on his shoulder.

"What was her name?"

"Nina."

"And?"

"Is that your third question?"

She nudged him with her knee. "Of course it's not my third question. We're still on number two. You can't just give me one-word answers. What happened?"

"That's question number three. She married someone else."

"Oh. I'm sorry. No one should have to go through that."

"Obviously, we weren't meant to be."

Caitlyn was quiet for a moment. "Yeah, that happens sometimes. I suppose it's better to discover it before you marry the person rather than afterward."

Her right hand had found its way onto his thigh. She nearly drove him crazy the way she traced small circles on his leg with her forefinger.

His skin prickled under her touch.

"Is Nina the one who convinced you that you don't have a heart?"

He shrugged and coughed out a laugh. "If I had a pound for every time someone told me I was heartless, I'd be the wealthiest man in the world."

"Don't skirt the question. Did she?"

"She did, as did many others. Does it really matter?"

"Yes, it matters, because they were wrong. You're not as heartless as you would like everyone to believe, Brodie. I've glimpsed that heart of yours when you didn't know I was looking. You don't have to pretend with me."

The heartrending tenderness in her eyes.

His body ached for her.

He wasn't sure who moved first, but they went from zero to sixty in a heartbeat. His lips were on hers, and she gasped a little. The sound she made was nearly silent—more of a shudder than a sound. Brodie wondered if maybe he'd *felt* rather than heard her. But it didn't matter. The important thing was she didn't pull away; she didn't break contact.

They shouldn't be doing this—for so many reasons. But she was kissing him back and he wanted to devour her like a starving man at a sumptuous buffet.

Their kiss sent him reeling back to that first night. It nearly took him over the edge as new spirals of ecstasy unfurled in his body. Heat stirred and pooled in his groin as his body responded. He couldn't remember when he'd needed a woman as badly—as desperately— as he needed Caitlyn Moore.

He had no idea how long the two of them were up there tangled up in each other's arms because for a beautiful while, time vanished, and they were the only people in the universe. The only thing that brought Brodie back to reality was the jolt of a deafening alarm that sliced through the bliss and broke the two of them apart.

Caitlyn blinked at him as if she were gathering her faculties. Then her eyes flew open wide. "Hang on. This thing is about to start again."

He stole one more kiss.

With his lips a hair away from hers, he assured her, "I can guarantee you it already has."

Chapter Nine

It was a hell of a long walk back to the office. They took care to keep a respectable amount of distance between them. Caitlyn was too quiet. So Brodie knew it was up to him to break the ice.

"I hope Truvy left before the malfunction."

"That would be a lucky break," Caitlyn said.

Once they were back on the ground, trying to act normal—as normal as one could after making out atop a stalled roller coaster—the second thing they asked was what time the reporter had left.

The first question was, of course, "What the hell happened?"

Les didn't know what caused the malfunction, but he assured them he would get to the bottom of it in short order. But when it came to info about Truvy, he wasn't so helpful.

"She was here snapping pictures when the ride blasted off, but I couldn't tell you how long she stayed after the thing started malfunctioning."

"Did she realize it broke down?" Caitlyn asked.

Les shrugged. "I couldn't tell you how long she hung around. I was working. But I don't see her around here now. If you'll excuse me, I need to get back to work."

Brodie decided if Truvy had witnessed the malfunction, she would've waited around to ask questions. No need to worry when it probably would turn out to be nothing.

"Right, Les," Brodie said. "Please let us know when you figure out what went wrong with the ride and when you think it will be good to go. We're only a few days away from opening. We need to make sure everything is shipshape."

Les nodded curtly and turned away.

He'd given no indication that he or anyone else on the ground was any wiser to what had been going on high up there on the apex of that final hill. On one hand, he knew behavior like that wasn't professional, but on the other hand Caitlyn was all that mattered.

Since that day when he'd walked into the Cowboy Country USA offices and saw her standing there, he'd been fighting these feelings.

He'd been grasping at any reason to prove that they were not good together.

But *why*?

Ever since Nina he'd buried himself in his work.

With the exception of a few casual relationships, he hadn't allowed himself to look away from work long enough to see what was good or right or true about love.

Or maybe he'd been waiting for the right person to lift him out of his slump.

As they passed Gulch Holler Rapids log flume ride, Brodie stole a glance at Caitlyn.

Is she the right person?

Was she the one or was he telling himself that to make himself feel better about getting involved with Alden Moore's daughter?

He felt himself wanting to backpedal, but he recognized that traditionally, this was where the walls would go up, and he would slip out the side door.

Then he rode it out and after the wave broke, his feelings for her were still standing.

They didn't have to rush things, but he didn't want to delay things, either.

Caitlyn paused outside the entrance to their building.

"Do you really think we're going to be ready to open Memorial Day?" she asked. Even if we have to delay a week or two, don't you think that's better than running the risk of something like this happening with guests in the park?"

"If the Twin Rattlers isn't ready to go, we don't have to run it. But we do have to open the park as promised. It's in my contract."

"I don't have a contract—"

Brodie leaned in and silenced her with a kiss.

"What are we doing?" Worry clouded her eyes.

"Are you talking about business or—" He motioned back and forth between them.

She gave a quick one-shoulder shrug, and he knew exactly what she was talking about.

He smiled at her. "I'd show you, but I don't know if it would set a very good example if someone walked around the corner and saw me ravishing you right here. They might have to fire both of us."

"Yeah, about that. It probably wasn't the smartest idea to make out on a roller coaster in the middle of the park. Although, I must admit, I've always wanted to do that."

Brodie feigned surprise. "What? The Princess of Coaster World has never made out on a roller coaster? I'm your first?"

"Yes. Given that it's the first time I've ever been stuck on a roller coaster. They're not exactly the tunnel of love when they're going at full speed."

"Touché."

She caught her top lip between her teeth and looked up at him, emotion darkening her eyes.

"I'm not cut out for flings," she said. "That woman who ravaged you at the wedding wasn't me. I mean, it was *me*, obviously, but I'm not like that. I've never picked up a stranger before. So I don't want you to have the wrong impression. Although, I guess it's too late for that."

Color rose in her cheeks as she rolled her eyes. He loved how flustered she got sometimes when she tried to explain herself.

Now more than ever he wanted to pull her into his arms.

He opened his mouth to tell her so, but she silenced him by raising her hand.

"I want you to think about it. You don't have to give me an answer right now—right here. This isn't really the time or the place to decide something so personal."

A smile tugged up the corners of his lips. "I agree. So why don't you have dinner with me tonight, and we can talk about it when we have more privacy?"

Janie held out a piece of paper to Caitlyn as she and Brodie made their way back to their offices.

"Ms. Moore, Truvy Jennings from the newspaper called for you. She says she needs more information about the Twin Rattlers for the article she's writing. I told her that you and Mr. Fortune Hayes were still out in the park, and she asked if y'all were still having problems with the ride. Is there a problem?"

Caitlyn and Brodie exchanged an alarmed glance, but Janie's expression was earnest as she looked back and forth between the two of them.

"What did you say to her, Janie?" Caitlyn put on her professional smile and did her best to make sure the panic crawling up the back of her throat didn't croak through in her voice.

"I told her I didn't know. That you and Mr. Fortune Hayes were just out in the park like you always are and I wasn't aware of anything being wrong."

Caitlyn's alarm slipped a couple of notches.

"You did the right thing, Janie, thank you," said Brodie. "This is not a reprimand. It's simply a directive for the future because it's likely we will be receiving more calls from media outlets from all over the world in the next couple of weeks. But it's important that no one speak to the media except for Ms. Moore and myself. In a case like this, when someone starts asking questions, simply tell them that you'd be happy to take a message. Do you understand?"

Janie nodded. "I did take a message, and she wants you to call her back. Her number is on the paper."

As they made their way down the hall, Brodie said, "I'll take care of Truvy."

Caitlyn handed him the number and quirked a brow. "She'd probably rather talk to you, anyway. Work your charm."

Brodie took her proffered paper with Truvy's number. "But before I take care of this, how about if I make us a seven-thirty reservation at the Cantina?"

"That sounds wonderful," she said.

Brodie pulled her inside his office and covered her mouth with a kiss.

When Caitlyn came up for air, she pulled back and looked at him with dreamy eyes.

"We really do have to stop doing that at work. Janie might walk in without knocking."

Brodie narrowed his eyes at her. "I thought Janie usually buzzed you when she needed you."

"Well, yeah, there's that, but you never know when she might surprise us and walk in."

Brodie reached out and picked up a strand of Caitlyn's hair and started twirling it around his finger.

"Go," Caitlyn said. Make our dinner reservation and then make us look good for Truvy. In the meantime, I'm going to finish up the outline for the Red, White and Blue team days."

The workers had been divided into three groups of Red, White and Blue teams, and they would each have a day where they could bring a guest to enjoy themselves in the park. Afterward, each person would come to a debriefing meeting and rate their experience. It was like a soft, soft opening, with a report card, done by the workers out on the front lines. They'd use this exercise to work out the first kinks. The exercise was also designed to make the employees buy into this sense of ownership and experience firsthand the expectations of Moore Entertainment.

Brodie came in to tell her about his call with Truvy, which had been pretty standard—she had seen the roller coaster stall and wanted to know if that would have an impact on the park's opening. He told her absolutely not.

He had other news for Caitlyn, too. His aunt Jeanne Marie called and asked them if they could stop by around five-thirty. She wanted to talk to them about their plan to get on the agenda for next week's town meeting. There was no time to waste and since Brodie's aunt had made time for them, Caitlyn certainly wanted to meet with her while they had the chance. Who knew if she would have time before the meeting?

Besides, their reservation at the Cantina wasn't until later. Of course, meeting with Jeanne Marie meant that Caitlyn wouldn't have time to go home and freshen up before dinner, but hearing what Jeanne Marie had to say was more important.

By five-thirty they were sitting at the trestle table in Jeanne Marie's spacious kitchen.

"Where's Mum and everyone else?" Brodie asked.

Jeanne Marie had brewed a pitcher of fresh sweet tea, which she served to them over ice, with lemon rounds and sprigs of aromatic fresh mint.

"Orlando Mendoza drove your mother to Lubbock because she had some shopping to do." Jeanne Marie lifted a brow. "She seems to have that man wrapped around her little finger these days."

"Yes, I noticed they seemed quite chummy at the barbecue," Brodie said. "What's going on there?"

Caitlyn sipped the cool beverage and realized she was a little nervous. The scent of the lemon and mint was soothing, but it didn't completely cure her jitters. This woman could help smooth the way for them… or not.

Never mind Caitlyn's personal plea about the place being so important to her ailing father, Jeanne Marie's own nephew was working so hard to make sure the park opened to rave reviews. Because of that alone, when Caitlyn had left the barbecue last week, she'd been under the impression that the Fortunes' hardline stance toward Cowboy Country had softened.

Caitlyn hadn't been surprised by their perceived change of heart.

Now she wasn't so sure, but she guessed they were about to find out.

"Who knows what's going on between them—if anything." Jeanne Marie sipped her tea. "Your mother insists they're just friends, but they're texting all the time like a couple of teenagers. It's ridiculous."

The corners of Brodie's eyes slanted Caitlyn a glance.

The left corner of his mouth curved up, and there were those dimples.

Her heart kicked up a little two-step as she remembered the way he'd kissed her senseless in the park today.

Oh, Caitlyn. Stop it. This woman could make or break your chances for time in front of the city council, and here you are lusting over her nephew. So inappropriate.

"But that's not why I asked you to come over here today," the older woman said. "We need to get down to business and talk about this plan of yours to speak to the city council. I have to leave here for my canasta club in a few minutes. I wish I could offer to make you some dinner, but I don't have time."

"That's okay, Auntie. I appreciate the thought, but we're going out to dinner after we leave here."

Jeanne Marie's face brightened. "Are you, really? Together? As in a dinner date?"

Brodie's brows knit together. "Let's stay on topic, shall we? Since you're pressed for time."

Jeanne Marie eyed Caitlyn and Brodie with satisfaction for a moment, before she became all business again. "So tell me, what exactly do you hope to accomplish by doing that?"

"We're tired of being the five-hundred-pound gorilla in the middle of the room that no one wants to talk about," Brodie said.

"Oh, they're all talking about you," Jeanne Marie said. "I'm just not so sure they want to talk *to* you."

Caitlyn's heart sank. "Forgive me if I'm being presumptuous, but I thought you'd changed your mind about Cowboy Country."

Jeanne Marie sighed and traced her fingernail over a grain in the wooden tabletop. "I understand where you're coming from and, if truth be told, I admire how this project is important to you because it's important to your daddy. The Fortunes are all about sticking up for family. However, it's not as simple as my liking it or not. The city council doesn't give a pig's snout about my opinion."

Brodie drummed his fingers on the table. "I don't believe that for one minute. You and Uncle Deke carry a lot of influence in this town. In fact, aren't a couple of the council members related to you…to us, I mean?"

Jeanne Marie nodded. "But they certainly don't come to me for counsel. If your plan is to go to the citizens of Horseback Hollow with your hat in your hand asking them to love you, I don't want you to be under the false assumption that their minds will be as easily changed as the family's."

Caitlyn knew she was grasping at straws, but had Jeanne Marie just admitted that she and the Fortunes— at least those in her immediate family—supported Cowboy Country? That's what she heard, and that's what she decided she was going to focus on…the positive.

"No, we're not going there asking them to love us," Caitlyn assured her. "Everything I said to you about wanting to be a good neighbor is absolutely sincere and true. What Brodie and I hope to accomplish in that meeting is we want to show them how we'll do that, how we can help. Cowboy doesn't want to take anything from Horseback Hollow. We want to give back to the community in the ways that I mentioned last week at dinner and even more."

Jeanne Marie's face gave nothing away as she studied them with blue eyes that were the same shade as Brodie's. Caitlyn idly wondered if triplets ran in Brodie's family.

Not that it mattered.

"I hope you can go in there and convey that same conviction," she said. "Because it's not going to be easy to win over everyone, but if anyone can do it, I believe you two can. So since the mayor has asked to hold this meeting in our barn out back because there are too many people for the Grill in town, I called in a favor. I asked him about the two of you doing a short presentation. He said for you to give his secretary a call and he will put you on the agenda for next Tuesday night."

It felt like another victory, Brodie thought as he drove toward Caitlyn's apartment in Vicker's Corners. He'd stopped at the Wok In Carry Out Chinese restaurant where he'd picked up takeout for them to share for dinner. Before that, he'd picked up a bottle of nice champagne. Because tonight was a night that called for some bubbly.

After they'd left Jeanne Marie's house, they'd decided to celebrate in a more casual atmosphere than the Cantina. When Caitlyn said she'd wanted to change into something more comfortable than the silk blouse and snug skirt she'd worn to work that day, he'd offered to pick up takeout and meet her at her place.

When she answered the door, the sight of her virtually knocked the breath out of him. She wore a pretty pink cotton sundress that even in its casualness hugged her in all the right places.

This thing between them was so new—well, it wasn't *new*; these feelings, this chemistry, hadn't gone away since the moment they'd met—but this renewal was fragile. Before he could overthink it, he decided to take the lead and kiss her hello. Standing there with his hands full of bags and the bottle, he leaned in and claimed her lips.

She wrapped her arms around his neck, and he held the parcels out to allow her to get closer. Blood pooled in the center of his body. Hot. Urgent. His senses screamed in a rush of want and need.

"I've been dying to do that again since we got down off that bloody ride this afternoon. Have I told you how much I love roller coasters?"

She laughed. "I thought you hated them."

His lips still on hers, he said, "I've been cured. The tunnel of love ain't got nothing on the Twin Rattlers."

She gently bit his bottom lip and sucked it before she said, "Come in. I don't want to put on a show for the neighbors."

When he stepped inside, he set the goods down on the wooden coffee table in the apartment's small living room. He pulled her to him again, wanting to feel every inch of her body pressed against his hardness. Needing to bury himself deep inside her.

She felt so right in his arms. All at once, all the uncertainty was replaced by a feeling so right, so profound he knew he had to have her.

All of her.

In Brodie's arms, Caitlyn's senses took flight. Or did they take leave?

She tried to think through the fuzzy haze that had invaded her brain. He smelled divine. That green and woodsy scent was so him. She breathed him in as he trailed kisses down her neck. That's when she gave up trying to make sense of it all and gave in to the rapture.

A moan of pleasure escaped from somewhere deep in her throat. Brodie ran his hands over her back, down the soft cotton of her sundress, until he gently cupped her bottom and pulled the center of her to the rock-hard center of him.

"I want you," he whispered.

The room tipped on end. She wondered if anyone had ever drowned in her own desire for a man.

"Caitlyn?"

"Mmm?"

"Is this okay? I mean, are you hungry?"

She smiled.

She nodded and buried her hands into his thick hair. "Yes, I'm so ravenous I don't even know where to begin. Here—"

She unbuttoned the top button of his shirt.

"Or here—" She slid her hand down his flat stomach and dipped her finger into the waistband of his pants.

"Let me help you with that decision."

He lifted her off the ground, cradling her in his

strong arms, and kissed her as he started walking toward her bedroom.

Her heart beat so wildly she was sure he could feel it. She couldn't remember a time when she hadn't longed for this moment because everything before him had faded away. She searched his eyes and answered him with a kiss that spoke of all the passion and certainty she felt.

Just inside the door, he adjusted the dimmer on the overhead light so that it glowed a warm, subtle glow. Just enough light to see. Barely.

Gently, he laid her on the bed.

She was going to make love with this gorgeous, sexy man who would probably leave right after the park opened and never come back. And yes, she would be devastated.

But tonight he was all hers. They had this moment. Right now.

Looming over her, he stripped off his shirt and tossed it away, onto the floor, then eased down beside her and propped himself up on one elbow.

From this vantage point he looked huge, all muscled chest and broad shoulders. She shuddered, needing to feel his bare skin pressed against her own.

He stroked her cheek and lowered his mouth to meet hers, his lips closing over hers soft and gentle at first, then more demanding.

His hand had worked its way up underneath her dress. His finger deftly slid under her bra and brushed over her breast. Those thoughts of him leaving that had plagued her a moment earlier melted away under his very skilled hands. Desire shot through every inch of her body, pooling in secret, vulnerable spots that had been starving for him for way too long.

He seemed to know precisely how to work the hook on her bra, because before she realized what he was doing, he'd tossed it away. She tried not to think about how many women he must have undressed to be that good at it. She hadn't had many lovers—none since Eric. But she'd hungered for Brodie the past few weeks, and any residual preoccupation left her mind as she focused on how tonight felt as if they were about to make love for the very first time. Well, for the second first time.

His hand on her breast sent tendrils of pleasure spiraling through her body. Brodie might be leaving soon, but she would show him how good they could be together, remind him how right they were for each other. He made her feel alive in a way she hadn't felt in a long time. She wanted to make him feel just as good.

Her finger traced the edge of his pants, where a line of fine hair disappeared into the waistband. She slid her palm down over the bulge just below it. He moaned.

Fumbling with the button on his pants, she finally worked it loose. She hesitated and looked up at him.

He reached down and worked her dress up and over her head and tossed it away.

"You're so beautiful." He looked at her body in a way that was positively reverent. He touched her face and then softly stroked her neck and the cleft between her breasts as he worked his way downward. When his lips sought out her nipple, she was gone. Utterly gone. Incoherent, lost in the feel of him on loving her body.

His kiss found her lips again, and his tongue slid into her mouth, as his knee nudged apart her thighs. When his hand found her center, even through her panties, the sensation made her back arch off the bed.

She freed his hard length from his pants and caressed him. He responded with a shuddered moan and eased his pants and underwear off in one easy motion. Then he straddled her and slid off her panties with equal ease.

She lay naked and vulnerable and ready for him.

He kissed her slow and deep for the longest time and when he finally pulled back, she heard the sound of a foil condom package opening. Impatient for him, desperate for him, she watched as he sheathed himself.

He settled himself on top of her, propping his upper body on his elbows. Stroking her hair, his lips found that tender spot where her neck curved into her ear then trailed kisses down her neck. He was about to drive her insane from the need, which had her body moving under him, straining, trying to get close.

One of his hands dipped between them. He shifted his weight, and she felt him positioning himself against her before he entered her body, filling her with an incredible rush of pleasure.

She gasped as fire burned through her veins to the very center of her womanhood. Arching against him, she grabbed on to his hips and threw her knees out as wide as they could go, needing to feel him all the way to her soul. He was sensuous and weighty, rolling on top of her, inside her, the friction of his body creating a growing heat. He gave her everything he had, pumping into her hard and deep until she cried out his name as waves of pleasure built. Swelled. Until she came completely unraveled and spiraling over the edge.

When she lay spent and pliable under him, his head fell to her shoulder, and his rhythm grew steadier, faster, until his entire body began to tremble. With a growl, he let go of his control and spilled everything he had.

Then there was stillness broken only by the sound of their breathing.

Chapter Ten

She thought making love to Brodie Fortune Hayes—again—would ruin everything she'd worked so hard to establish. But she was wrong.

It had never felt so wonderful to be wrong.

Things weren't awkward or strained. Instead, there was a heightened sense of synergy between them. The only challenge she found was keeping her mind on the job and out of the bedroom. And really, when she thought about it, it wasn't a challenge as much as it was the cherry on top.

They were so good together—both in the bedroom and out. And this intensified closeness helped on the night of the town council meeting.

Since the meeting was taking place in the barn on Deke and Jeanne Marie's property, Caitlyn thought those in attendance would be friendly—or at least open-minded. However, even though the Fortunes did wield some influence, it was clear that the folks of Horseback Hollow had minds of their own and would not be easily swayed.

She was amazed by how many people came clutching the newspaper with Truvy's story of the malfunctioning Twin Rattlers. With a headline reading Cowboy Country USA Off To Uncertain Start—Will Malfunctions Derail Memorial Day Opening?

Oh, Truvy, I thought you were on our side.

The reporter was seated in the front row, jotting notes in her reporter's notebook. She wouldn't make eye contact with Caitlyn. She wasn't sure if it was intentional or not. Everything seemed magnified right now.

Her gaze searched the room for Brodie, who was in the back helping serve the fresh lemonade and cookies that Jeanne Marie had provided. They had agreed that he would man that station, and she would work the other side of the room.

The only thing was that she was suddenly feeling a bit paralyzed and what looked like the entire town of Horseback Hollow filtered into the barn. From the looks of things, the crowd might be as large as it had been for the wedding. These good people took their town seriously.

Well, Caitlyn's convictions about Cowboy Country USA were just as strong and sincere. She wasn't here to mislead anyone. That truth would be the North Star that guided her through the evening.

Brodie was talking and shaking hands and doing

what he did best. He was with Cisco Mendoza and Delaney Fortune Jones. Caitlyn had met both of them when she and Brodie had arrived. Wonderful, warm people. Cisco looked animated and happy to be chatting with Brodie. That had to be a good sign, didn't it?

When Cisco left Cowboy Country everything began to unravel. As part of their strategy, Brodie had asked Cisco to stand up tonight and mention that the only problem he'd had with the project and the reason he'd left was because he felt the design didn't mesh with Horseback Hollow's landscape. The plan was that Brodie would assure the citizens that since then there had been a change in personnel, and that Moore Entertainment was discussing a more harmonious plan for the Cowboy Condos. A design that Cisco Mendoza himself had had a hand in bringing to life.

Of course, the unspoken message was Mendoza might have pulled out—and for good reason—but a Fortune had come on board and was fully endorsing the park. Not only was it good for the small town, but it was also economically beneficial.

Yes, Brodie was in his element. Caitlyn envied his ease, the way he seemed so comfortable in his own skin. Granted, he could be a little aggressive when he'd locked in on something he wanted—loyal employees, an iron-clad opening date, a lover—

Inappropriate. Stop it.

Caitlyn blinked away the thought and refocused on how, for the most part, Brodie Fortune Hayes knew how to win people over to his way of thinking. He was headstrong, and Caitlyn didn't agree with all his tactics, but she believed Brodie Fortune Hayes's heart was in the right place.

Good thing, because she feared she was losing her heart to him.

Stop, Caitlyn. Focus. And quit being a wallflower. Get out there and mingle. Do your job.

She knew she needed to, but it was easier said than done. Being at the center of a new situation wasn't her comfort zone. She liked to stand back and observe, get a read on a situation, absorb the vibe before she dove in. That's how her *gut* worked, and when she abided by it, she usually wasn't wrong.

However, today there wasn't a lot of time to stand back and assess. She would be doing herself a favor by meeting as many people as possible before she and Brodie got up to speak. They were the last on the agenda, and if she was anxious now, she knew her nerves would only get worse as the clock ticked closer and closer to their presentation.

She scanned the room for a friendly face, and her gaze connected with Susie Silverman, who was just entering the barn. Susie smiled back, waved and headed in her direction. Good thing she'd worn the cuff bracelet she'd purchased from Susie at the art festival. It wasn't just for show. She hadn't thought about currying favor when she'd slipped it on her wrist to complement the powder blue dress she'd chosen for the occasion— something soft and feminine, something that didn't scream city slicker, but still hinted that she was a professional and knew what she was doing.

All she knew was she loved the bracelet. It made her feel as if she were wearing a work of art.

"Hi, Caitlyn? Did I remember your name correctly?"

Caitlyn beamed at her. "You did, Susie. It's great to see you again."

"Hey, I *love* that bracelet." Susie reached out and lifted up Caitlyn's wrist. "You have impeccable taste, lady. I just finished making some earrings that would look great with it. Not too matchy-matchy, but close enough to harmonize."

"Save them for me. May I stop by your house next week to pick them up? I've wanted to come in and see you and your studio since the art festival. Life has just been a little crazy."

"I hear you. I understand you've had a full plate working toward the grand opening." Suzie gestured toward a newspaper that an older woman with jet-black hair was using as a fan. "Don't worry, though. People around here can be slow to embrace change, but most of them do eventually come around. I've lived here all my life, and I've seen it with my own two eyes. You'll be fine."

Susie waved at someone across the room. "There's Mary Jane Hardy. She's saved me a seat. Plus, it looks like the meeting is about to start. Knock 'em dead."

Susie would be one friendly face in the audience, in addition to Jeanne Marie and Deke, Josephine, Amelia and Quinn, Christopher Fortune Jones and his wife, Kinsley. Then there was Galen Fortune Jones, who could sometimes be a loose cannon, but surely tonight he would support his cousin or say nothing at all. Right?

She felt a hand on her shoulder and turned around to see Brodie. He handed her a small cup of lemonade and a fresh chocolate chip cookie on a red napkin. Caitlyn wondered if the napkin was left over from the wedding.

"Hungry crowd tonight. I saved these for you. Because until you've had Aunt Jeanne Marie's chocolate-chip cookies, you haven't lived."

"Thank you." As she reached to take the goodies, Brodie managed to squeeze her hand under the napkin. It was a private message that came with a smile that seemed to promise, *Don't worry. We've got this. Easy peasy.*

Although, she couldn't imagine that upright, handsome Brit actually saying *easy peasy.*

It really was a silly phrase. Yet the thought of it passing over those lips…*those lips…*

"What?" Brodie asked.

Caitlyn took a bite of the cookie. When she'd swallowed it, she said, "Delicious. That's what. Let's find our seats."

They sat with his family about midway back. Just far enough away to feel a little anonymous—though being the lone non-Fortune to sit with them probably made her stand out all the more. Still, being that far back allowed her to look around and spot some of the people who worked at the park. There was Janie, who must've slipped in just as they were starting because Caitlyn hadn't seen her earlier. And there was Les Campbell. And a group from food and beverage. But not as many as she would've thought.

Hmm…was that good or bad?

Caitlyn did her best to focus on the speakers, who stood on what looked like a modified version of the wedding stage. Before she knew it, it was time for Brodie and her to get up and deliver their piece. Before she stood, her throat went dry so she drank the last bit of lemonade, grateful for its tart coolness. They'd prepared a PowerPoint presentation, which was good because her mind was threatening to go blank right about now.

But all it took was one reassuring smile from Brodie, one touch of his hand as he helped her up the four wooden steps to the platform, and she caught her breath.

No need to be nervous. This is a win-win proposition.

Brodie went first, introducing her and giving the overview as he tried to get people excited. He worked through his part of the PowerPoint. Cisco stood at the appropriate moment and said the appropriate things. Still, something didn't feel right.

All this talk about designs and money flowing in from the outside through taxes and tourist spending seemed cold and…typical. Just a cordial way of saying, or not saying, like it or not Cowboy Country was here and really, there's nothing you can do about it.

"Now I'll turn the stage over to the lovely Caitlyn Moore, who will tell you about some wonderful incentives you're sure to find very exciting."

She gave Brodie a double take.

Incentives? That wasn't exactly the word she was going to use. Partners in business, maybe—

Brodie had done a good job presenting the facts, exactly as they'd discussed. But hearing it made it sound about as warm as a multilevel marketing plan. Not that there was anything wrong with multilevel marketing, but it wasn't for everyone, and rarely did it instill the warm fuzzies.

Caitlyn stepped up to the podium. Looked around and saw a mixture of emotions out there in the audience. She wasn't expecting to please everyone. So maybe she just needed to do what felt right to her.

"I want to tell you a personal story." Rather than following the PowerPoint, she began to speak from her heart. She told them the story of how her father started Moore Entertainment with one hundred dollars he'd saved from working an early-morning paper route when he was in high school. She told them he has always believed that being part of a community is so important. He learned that on his paper route. He knew the name of every single person on his route.

"He hasn't had a chance to meet all of you yet, because he's been having health problems, but just give him a chance and you'll know him like family."

She told them how he loves John Wayne and that Cowboy Country USA was a dream come true.

"It's not just another amusement park in the Moore Entertainment portfolio. This is personal. And out of all the places in the world, he chose Horseback Hollow. He wants to be part of this community, and he would be the one standing here telling you that if he weren't in a rehabilitation center in Lubbock, recovering. I almost lost my father. I think you can help give him a reason to live."

The air in the room seemed to change. Everyone sat quietly watching her.

"But me telling you the Cowboy Country story is only a fraction of why I'm here. I want to tell you how Moore Entertainment will be good neighbors to you, and I will not leave here until I have answered every one of your questions."

A hand shot up—a guy in the second row who didn't look entirely convinced.

"Okay, I have a question for you. According to the newspaper, you're having trouble getting your rides to work. As far as I'm concerned, the only thing worse than having an amusement park in my backyard is having a broken-down eyesore that doesn't work. I'm afraid we're going to be stuck with a theme-park ghost town if Moore Entertainment can't get its act together then pulls up stakes and leaves town."

Thanks, Truvy.

"What's your name, sir?" Caitlyn asked.

"Rodney Young."

"Mr. Young, I can assure you that Moore Entertainment would never leave you with a broken-down eyesore. We are still a couple of weeks away from opening our doors. We are testing equipment and fine-tuning everything around the park to have it ready and working for opening day. To put your mind at ease, I would like to invite you and your family to be our guest at the park on opening day. Come out and enjoy the park and see for yourself."

A wave of murmurs rippled through the audience.

Caitlyn smiled at him. Rodney Young sat up in his chair and arched his brows in a way that wasn't entirely bad.

"Well, thank you, ma'am. I'll take you up on that offer. How do I get in touch with you?"

"You can call me in the Cowboy Country offices anytime. In fact, that goes for all of you. I want to give every resident of Horseback Hollow a ticket for free park admission on opening day."

The crowd murmured again. Brodie put his hand on Caitlyn's arm. She glanced at him and through his smile he was giving her a *look*. It flashed in his eyes for just a moment—a *what the hell are you doing* look—but she ignored him.

"After that, we will offer you deeply discounted resident passes. All you have to do is show your ID with a Horseback Hollow address, and we will have a special rate."

"Could you please give us that number to the Cowboy Country offices?"

Her gaze picked out Janie in the audience. She looked horrified. But Caitlyn was as good as her word. She gave out the number.

Now Brodie's hand was on her back, and he was subtly moving into the microphone.

"Yes, one free ticket for everyone." He choked on the last word, but he quickly recovered. "For the day of the opening. Right. We will all have a lovely time. But getting back on track, there's more about how we would like to help Horseback Hollow's economy. To that end, Moore Entertainment would like to partner with local businesses who are interested in offering food and goods for sale within the park."

Getting back on track? What?

Granted, she had varied from the PowerPoint, and he didn't seem thrilled about her surprise offer of free admission on opening day, but that wasn't his decision to make. Common sense dictated that if they involved the residents of Horseback Hollow, the residents would see for themselves and soften their stance.

She put her hand on his back to signal that she would take it from here and tried to lean into the microphone to finish her part of the presentation, but he didn't budge.

And he kept talking.

So she did the only thing she could to get his attention without making a scene. She slid her hand down to his backside and pinched him.

"Yah!" he blurted.

Well, he deserved it. Edging me out like that.

Maybe it wasn't the most professional thing to do, but the podium was wide enough that nobody would've been the wiser, and her body blocked the view of those who were seated to the side of the stage—and had she mentioned he deserved it?

Caitlyn was a tolerant woman. But one of the things that pushed her hot button like no other was when a man tried to override her in business, treating her like a senseless little lady.

"Yes, Brodie. I'm excited about being a part of the Horseback Hollow community, too," she said in her cheeriest voice. "To pick up on what Brodie was saying, we will offer competitive compensation and make sure park guests are aware that each partner—vendor—is local by supplying signage and encouragement to visit your shop in the downtown area. Brodie and I will be making our way into different businesses in the downtown area to meet you and see how Cowboy Country can partner with you to promote your business, but if anyone has immediate interest, please feel free to see either of us before we leave tonight."

"What in the bloody world was that?" Brodie asked as soon as they were in the car. Actually, the question covered a litany of *bloody worlds*. He'd wanted to say *bloody hell*, but he'd managed to restrain himself. Because he was in the presence of a lady—even if she had pinched his arse in public and given away opening day of park attendance.

"Yes, I could ask you the same thing. What in the bloody world was that?" she asked. "Why did you butt into my part of the presentation? I was handling it."

Her green eyes looked about as wild as he felt. If he hadn't been so angry he might've noticed how sexy she looked when she was mad. But why the hell was *she* mad? She'd given everything away and gotten away with it.

"I didn't butt in, I simply steered you back on track. I understand you were nervous, but that's why we had the PowerPoint presentation." He softened his voice. "Why in the world did you not just stick to the plan we had agreed on?"

She glared at him for a moment that seemed to last an eternity.

"Because the plan may have worked on paper, but we were losing them. Couldn't you see that? We were coming to them with our hats in our hands, asking them to love us, as Jeanne Marie so aptly put it. We are the ones who are encroaching on their territory, changing the face of their community. It was our place to make a magnanimous gesture, and I stand by the offer. I just can't believe you are so blind you can't see it."

"You're right, I have been blind. I've been blinded by emotions that have no business in the workplace. Caitlyn, I signed a contract agreeing to open a profitable park, and you need to know that's what I intend to do."

Chapter Eleven

It was exactly what Caitlyn had feared would happen.

She and Brodie had been distant for days—since their disagreement after the town meeting.

How had it all snowballed out of control?

She'd thought about broaching the subject, but the way he'd been avoiding her made her feel so vulnerable that she always pulled back when she got the urge to reach out. Reaching out meant tracking him down. Reaching out meant pushing herself on a man who obviously had only been in it for fun—oh, and for business.

Business always took precedence.

She refused to let herself think that she could've loved this man.

No. She wasn't going to think about that.

So they continued to avoid each other in the name of

hard work. They both stayed so busy they didn't have to talk about what happened—or wasn't happening—between them.

Of course, there was so much to do in the time leading up to the park's opening that they hadn't had a moment to spare—or share a meal or kiss, certainly not make love. If things got any colder between them, they'd be at a risk for frostbite.

But there was too much to do right now to worry about that. Today was the start of the Red, White and Blue Extravaganza, an event to celebrate the employees' completion of the training program Brodie had created to get everyone "on the same page."

Caitlyn was busy looking over schedules to make sure all of the areas would be covered during the pre-opening employee event.

The Red, White and Blue Extravaganza was a peer review/fun day for each of the employees. Everyone who worked for Cowboy Country USA had been split into one of three groups—red, white and blue. Over the next three days each group would take turns enjoying the park and reviewing their peers' job performance.

Of course, nothing could just be fun when Brodie had a hand in it. Caitlyn had tried to get him to lay off, to let the workers enjoy a day of pure fun in the park that he so desperately wanted them to love. But the unspoken message seemed to be if they didn't buy into Cowboy Country heart and soul he would fire them.

Each day closer to the Memorial Day opening, Brodie seemed to get more intense, and Caitlyn's sinking feeling of impending disaster was nearly overwhelming. Just to keep the peace, she had decided she needed to choose her battles.

That was why she stepped back from taking the hard line on the setup of the Red, White and Blue Extravaganza. Maybe the peer review process would work. Personally, she thought it was a lot of weight to place on the employees' shoulders. Thank goodness, one thing Brodie had agreed to was that the reviews would be anonymous. The last thing they needed right now was for Carl over at the Runaway Stagecoach ride to find out that Karen over in the General Store had dinged him for lousy service.

Brodie's stance was that good service was good service and bad service was costly. The employees from top to bottom needed to get into the habit of providing good customer service even when they thought no one was looking.

Okay, he had a point. Of course she wanted Cowboy Country to provide the best possible experience for the guests, but there had to be another way to inspire the workers rather than put the fear of hanging in their hearts.

One of the things that she found the most distressing was that she thought she had recovered the Brodie she met that night of the Fortune wedding—her romantic, funny, kind, considerate astronomy nerd. But Brodie the Dictator had materialized again, eclipsing Brodie the Astronomy Nerd.

Did the guy have a split personality? Or an evil twin?

Now Caitlyn understood why it was difficult for couples to work together. The power struggles were killer.

Someone had to be the boss, and someone had to be bossed around.

If this project weren't so important to her father, she would just as soon go back to her office and research in Chicago and leave big business to the cutthroats.

Animals didn't talk back to you. If you respected them, for the most part they respected you. It was the truth, but she found it depressing. She'd been having visions lately of growing old surrounded by a zoo park of animals, but without a husband and family to love her.

That was why she couldn't quit now. She needed to stick with this project and see it through until the end. Maybe it was even more important to prove to herself that she could do it than it was to prove it to her father.

It was hard to keep her thoughts on the schedule. She found herself getting to the bottom of the page and having to admit that she hadn't comprehended what she'd read. Did she need to schedule two or three in the Lazy River Shootout? And was that for the day the White team or the Blue team would be hitting the park?

Ugh, she needed to go back and check. The last thing she needed was to mess this up.

She was scrolling through the computer file with the schedule when her cell phone rang.

She was tempted to let it go to voice mail, but then she saw her father's number displayed on the screen.

"Hi, Dad. Is everything okay?"

"It couldn't be better. I'm in the car right now, and your mother is driving me home from that godforsaken rehab center. I am a free man. Looks like I'll probably

be able to attend the opening ceremony on Memorial
Day. You have planned a ribbon-cutting, haven't you?"

"Yes, of course we have. This is such wonderful
news. When I spoke with Mom yesterday, she didn't
tell me you were being released today."

"It wasn't finalized until I saw the doctor today. She
didn't want to mention it in case it didn't happen. But
I knew it would. Hey, listen—" He must've held the
phone away from his mouth because what he said next
was a little muffled. It sounded something like, "I need
to discuss this with her, Barbara, but I'm not getting
upset. See, I'm perfectly calm. I can discuss business
and keep a level head."

His voice was clear again. "So what's this I hear
about you giving the entire town of Horseback Hollow
free admission on opening day?"

Great. Just great. The only way he could have
learned about that was through Brodie.

"Dad, it made sense. We don't have many fans in
the town— Well, we didn't. But now I think people are
starting to come around. We need to be good neighbors,
and this was the best way to do it. We had to be the first
ones to invite them to our *house*. It's amazing how far
a little goodwill will take you."

Her dad made a noise on the other end of the phone
that sounded like, *hummm*, before he said, "Well, no
skin off my nose. I'll take the revenue loss out of the
bonus based on opening day sales that I was going to
pay Hayes. That way we should break even. And if
your theory holds true, we may even come out on top
a little bit."

So that was why Brodie was so mad at her. Giving away tickets meant money out of his own pocket. She shouldn't have been surprised, but she was. He was a business consultant. Business consultants earned a handsome reward for pulling off miracles. Still, the reality of it burned a little.

"I appreciate you being my eyes and ears while I've been laid up. You know, taking time out of your own research to hold down the fort for your old man. Your being there has given me more peace than I've had in weeks. Months, maybe. Since you've made the sacrifice, after everything is up and running at Cowboy Country, we will seriously revisit those plans for that zoo park you've wanted for so long."

Caitlyn blinked. Was this her father speaking? Had those words just come out of his mouth?

"Of course, Dad. It's the least I could do. You needed me."

"Well, I need you to keep working with Hayes. Follow his lead. No more surprises, okay? I need that park to open on Memorial Day. If anyone can pull off this opening, he can."

Ah, okay. There it was.

His words were like a sucker punch.

She was the eyes and ears. Brodie was the brilliant mastermind.

She wanted to ask him, *What about inviting the town to the park?* That was her idea.

Despite the fact that he was a Fortune, *she* was the one who'd made inroads with the locals—well, okay, maybe by virtue of his birth they'd had an easier time getting on the town meeting agenda. But again, *town meeting—her idea.*

But there was no time to sulk or demand credit. What would it get her, anyway? A medal? A bonus? Respect?

Hardly.

In her father's eyes she was the dutiful daughter. That role did not command respect. Love, yes.

Respect, no.

She had a vision of her mother, the epitome of the proper wife, who was always at her husband's side. She made life nice for her husband and for Caitlyn, too—arranging her life around them. It had never dawned on her until now how much of herself her mother had sacrificed.

Was this the way she'd imagined her life would turn out?

More important, was she happy? Or was there something else she was capable of that might have made her so much happier? At this point, she might never know.

Because of the subservient role her mother had always played to her father, it had always been important to Caitlyn to be her own person. To know what she wanted and what she was capable of and to go out and get it. That was why she'd broken the engagement to Eric. He'd cheated. If she'd looked the other way, that wouldn't have just been subservient, that would've been selling herself short, giving him permission to disrespect her. Because she knew she wanted and deserved so much more.

She wasn't going to let anyone bring her down or make her feel less about herself.

So why couldn't she tell her father that she'd played so much more of a role in the park's success than he realized?

Searching for the words, she opened her mouth to tell him, but all she ended up doing was sucking in a breath to fill in the cracks that were starting to form in her bravado.

"Don't worry, Dad."

"I'm not. Because I know that you know that the best medicine you could give me would be a park that's up and running."

And what was she supposed to say to that?

It was exactly what Brodie had feared would happen. Even if they needed to keep things strictly business, he'd hoped that they could at least be friends.

For two weeks, they'd been running at opposite ends, only discussing business matters. Strictly avoiding all things personal.

She'd gone rogue on him.

She'd cost him his bonus.

She'd cost him his mind.

But the thing that scared him the most was when he realized he *had* given up the bonus for her by not over-riding her off-the-cuff offer of free admission for the residents of Horseback Hollow.

He could've done it. Alden Moore had assigned him the authority to do whatever it took to get that park open and off to a profitable start.

He could have vetoed her getaway.

The only reason he hadn't disputed Caitlyn was because he hadn't wanted to embarrass her in front of the entire town of Horseback Hollow.

And that meant he was going soft.

He never should have kissed her atop that stalled roller coaster. He certainly never should have made love to her that night and then spent most of the next week with her, but it had felt so right. Obviously, his brain had been addled.

It's just that no matter where he was with Caitlyn, it seemed to feel like home, and here they were the day before the opening, and they were still at odds with each other.

It was probably for the best—as long as it didn't get in the way of business. He would be leaving soon. He'd been away from the London office for far too long. This project had been so demanding there was no way he was going to leave here without another success neatly cataloged for Hayes Consulting.

He realized with a start that he'd neglected to book his plane ticket home. He'd have to ask Janie to do that for him when he got back into the office. Right now he had matters to tend to. He needed to do a final walk-through to make sure everything was in place for tomorrow.

Actually, he and Caitlyn should be doing this walk-through together. Today he'd only caught glimpses of her here and there as she bustled about taking care of the matters that had turned up during the three days of the Red, White and Blue Extravaganza.

He silently congratulated himself for coming up with such an interactive plan that gave the employees reason to take ownership. Of course a few feathers had been ruffled in the process of smoothing things out, but this was no time for the rank-and-file to take things personally. He needed everyone to take things seriously. If that meant losing those who refused to do so, well, so be it.

They'd only lost five employees in the process—three had gotten upset and quit when he'd gone to them with the tickets their peers had filled out detailing gum chewing, slow service and basic incompetence. He'd had to fire two: one woman had taken a two-hour lunch break, but had only clocked out for a half hour; and a guy who'd worked in the General Store had eaten a pound of fudge without paying for it. Caitlyn had taken issue with his decision about letting the guy go. She'd sided with him because he had claimed there was a certain amount of fudge to be given out as samples. No one had told him he could not indulge. So he'd eaten an entire pound over the span of one shift. Right in front of his coworkers.

Apparently, no one told him taking candy without paying for it was stealing.

Caitlyn had argued that they should do a better job at making the rules clear. Since they hadn't communicated properly, she thought the guy should be given a second warning. But Brodie had used his veto power and insisted that they make an example of the guy. It would be a lesson that the entire workforce could learn from.

Caitlyn had looked at him as if he were a monster and simply walked away. But not before she said, "It's your conscience. This one is on you."

Damned if that little dig didn't hit home, because it seemed as if she had delivered it with a double meaning.

She was right, actually, about the personal part. The second time they'd made love *was* on his conscience. He should've known better. He'd broken his own rule of not getting involved with clients.

Now he was paying the price.

Brodie stopped to inspect a stack of T-shirts that had been haphazardly plopped on a four-sided shelving unit at the front of one of the gift shops. He was just about to call one of the shop attendants over so that he could demonstrate the correct way to fold and display merchandise, when Caitlyn walked around the corner and nearly ran into him.

"There you are," she said. "I've been looking for you."

His stomach dropped before he'd had a chance to put up his guard. He had to be careful because the woman had that effect on him.

"You could've called me," he said and immediately regretted it because it sounded so personal. He straightened his shoulders—he certainly hadn't meant it to be personal. Although he did miss talking to her. He missed their banter, the way she challenged him.

Well, actually, he didn't miss being challenged. Not at work. But what little leisure time he'd had over the past two weeks had been quite dull since the two of them had taken a step back.

Of course, he'd been so busy all he'd have time for was to grab food on the go and fall into bed at night, exhausted—and alone.

In his weakest moments he missed holding her, he

missed the way she fit so perfectly into his arms, and he missed her smell. How could he have grown so fond of someone after only a week of intimacy? Well, really this thing had been brewing since the wedding in February. But back then he never thought he'd see her again. Now even the thought of their nights together had him breathing in a little deeper as she stood in front of him.

Today, her long, dark hair was twisted off her neck. She wore a green blouse that skimmed her curves and brought out the emerald shade of her eyes. And apparently she'd just asked him a question, and he had no idea what she'd said.

"Brodie, did you hear me?"

His blank look must've said it all because she frowned and said, "I've been over at the Wild West Show for the past hour, and things are not going well. During rehearsal, the horses weren't cooperating. One keeps raring up and the others just seem spooked. It seems that the horses are not adapting. They're still getting spooked by the gunshot sounds."

"What happened? Everything was going so well. I thought they had all the kinks worked out."

"Well, they don't. Some of the horses are acting very skittish. They might need more time to adjust to the sound of the gunshots in the show. I know you're not going to like this, but since the Twin Rattlers ride is still not operational and now with the kinks in this show—those are two of our biggest attractions. I think we need to delay the opening until we have everything under control. Or at least delay the opening of the Wild

West Show. My gut is telling me we're not even ready for a soft opening."

"Come on, let's walk look over there," Brodie suggested. His sister-in-law-to-be, Amber Rogers, was in the show. If anyone knew horses, it was Amber. She was a professional-level rider. She'd won rodeos, exemplified grace under pressure. If anyone could help them make this work, Amber could do it.

Caitlyn was a bundle of nerves. He could see it in her face, in the absence of her smile, the set of her jaw. The urge to pull her into his arms and kiss away all the tension that was etched in her beautiful face was nearly overpowering.

And it was further proof that he needed to keep his distance.

"I just don't see how we can delay, Caitlyn. We have media from all over the country lined up to tour the park, and we can't postpone at this late date. That in and of itself would guarantee the worst type of publicity. Not to mention, there is the small fact that we have all those comp tickets outstanding. Explain that one to the community."

He couldn't look at her. It was a jerky thing to say—even if it was the truth—and his voice sounded harsher than it should have. He hated himself for it. Yet he couldn't seem to stop pushing her away.

"So under no circumstances will we delay the scheduled opening. The purpose of a *soft* opening is that it's a *dress rehearsal*—a chance to work through the kinks."

"I understand what you're saying," she said. "But in a sense, this will be the *fourth* dress rehearsal since we had three days of practice with the Red, White and Blue teams, and we still don't have our act together. Don't you think the bad publicity derived from opening before we're ready will be worse than if we postpone?"

He shook his head. "We will just have to push through this and not let nerves get the best of us."

She stopped and put her hands on her hips. "So this is what it comes down to? You're the one with all the power? You're the one who makes the final call? I get no say in what happens to my father's business?"

"I am simply abiding by the letter of the contract that I have with your father. My reputation is at stake here, Caitlyn. I have to do what I think is best. I can't manage by my gut—there's no room in business for that. I have to go by facts and figures. I'm sorry."

"Wow. Thanks for that." He could almost see the anger radiating off her in waves. "Let's go see that Wild West show. Maybe you'll be able to pick up some additional tips on other ways to ride roughshod over anyone who gets in your way."

This is why you don't get involved, man.

Maybe if he said that to himself enough, he would be able to apply it to Caitlyn.

Deep inside a voice said, *Nope. Not going to happen.*

He had an idiotic flash of fantasy that maybe after all the madness was over they could talk things out and try to make things work. But then reality came crashing down. He'd go back to Hayes Consulting's headquarters in London, and she would go back to her research in Chicago. Neither one could give up their lives for the other.

"You know, I'm not doing this to hurt you," he said. "This is business, Caitlyn. This is not personal. Your father has certain expectations. And I need his endorsement for a potential project I hope to line up down the road."

"Let's just go watch the show," Caitlyn said, bitterness in her tone. "Don't patronize me."

They walked in silence to the ring that housed the Wild West Show. Even before they got there they could hear the horses whinnying and snorting. And it didn't sound good.

The director, Tom, nodded as he saw Caitlyn and Brodie approach the sidelines.

"Places, everyone," he said to the performers. "Let's take it from the top."

When everybody was on their marks, the director called, "Action!"

Even as the riders began to steer their horses into place, Brodie could see that some of the talent was having difficulty. Some of the animals seemed skittish and uncomfortable.

"Cut! Cut!"

Brodie leaned over and whispered, "Do we have other horses we could try instead of the ones that are so nervous?"

"We do have backups, but don't you think the director and the animal trainers have already thought of that?"

"So basically what you're saying is we're stuck with these animals? We have to make it work?"

"The backup horses might work if we altered the

show, or at least that's what Tom was telling me." Caitlyn motioned toward the director, who was sitting in a chair on the side of the ring. "But even so, it would call for new routine blocking and new rehearsals to get everything down. Brodie, what you don't seem to understand is that these are *animals*. Sometimes they don't follow orders. They are often unpredictable, and sometimes no matter how you try you cannot control them. They have feelings and minds of their own."

Feelings?

The way she was looking at him, tempted him to ask if she was talking about the animals or...them. But then a gunshot blasted, and the big white stallion that Amber was riding reared up onto its back legs, came down hard, lost its balance, throwing Amber.

Demonstrating her experience, Amber Rogers managed to throw her small body in the opposite direction of the giant animal.

"Amber! Are you okay?" Everyone shouted the words at the same time and rushed over to tend to her. But she didn't pay any attention. All she wanted to do was get to her horse and soothe him.

Amber was visibly upset, and Caitlyn hurried over to comfort her.

All Brodie could hear was bits and pieces of what they were saying.

"I know," Caitlyn said. "I told him..." The tones of the conversation drifted lower, and he couldn't hear the rest of what they were saying, but he was certain they weren't saying nice things about him and his decision to open as scheduled with as many full shows running as possible.

Brodie dragged his hand over his face. He was beginning to question his decision—but still believed that opening on schedule was in Moore Entertainment's best interests. And Brodie never failed to do as he promised. Still…

He walked over to Amber and Caitlyn. "Are you okay, Amber?"

"I'm fine, but I'm worried about my horse," Amber said, visibly upset. "Brodie, I have to second what Caitlyn is suggesting about not opening the show tomorrow. We aren't ready and the horses still need to get acclimated—"

"I'll tell you what," Brodie said. "You go ahead and keep rehearsing, and we will see how things are tomorrow."

Amber nodded but didn't look much happier. But Brodie had to commend her for being a team player.

He might be the most unpopular guy in Cowboy Country right now, but they were going to open this park on time. Because he had already bet the good name of Hayes Consulting on it.

Chapter Twelve

With the cut of a giant red ribbon stretched across the Cowboy Country USA gates, the park was officially open for business.

And it had opened on time.

Brodie breathed a giant sigh of relief as he and Caitlyn shook hands with the mayor of Horseback Hollow, the town council and a frail-looking Alden Moore, who had come for the opening ceremony.

"Did you see that crowd gathered outside the gates this morning?" he asked Alden, who had given the opening address, thanking the citizens of Horseback Hollow for making this day possible and, with Caitlyn's help, had done the honor of cutting the ribbon with the giant gold-painted scissors.

"I did," Alden said. "I did, indeed. Hayes, you did a fabulous job. Worth every penny I spent on you."

The older gentleman laughed, but it turned into a wheeze that turned into a coughing fit. He put a hand up to his chest and leaned on his daughter.

"Dad, I know this is a big day," said Caitlyn. "But you really shouldn't overdo it."

Caitlyn slanted a glance at her mother, who looked just as elegant as always, dressed in a feminine spring suit and pearls. Somehow the dressy ensemble didn't seem out of place at a cowboy-themed amusement park. Elegance and refinement seemed to run in the blood of Moore women.

Even Caitlyn, who was dressed in a crisp white button-down blouse tucked into low-slung khakis with a cordovan leather belt that lay just perfectly on her slim hips, looked effortlessly cool and chic.

Ah, hell. Who is he kidding? He had never seen anyone make a white Brooks Brothers button-down look downright sexy. His heart gave a regretful squeeze.

Brodie had to hand it to her. Yesterday she had been nearly overwrought with nerves and trepidation about opening the park today. Looking at her now, you would never know that she had been ready to reschedule everything. But her ability to be a team player and remain calm when it really mattered were two of the things that Brodie admired so much about her.

"Alden, I couldn't have pulled this off without your daughter."

And then the strangest thing happened. If looks could have killed, Caitlyn had pinned him with one meant to take his head off. She didn't say a word. She didn't need to; her expression said it all.

But what?

Why had she taken such offense?

Thank God, Truvy Jennings chose that moment to ask for a group photo. Caitlyn's beautiful features softened into her professional smile as Alden, Barbara, Caitlyn and he posed for the camera.

"Truvy, I'd like to introduce you to Alden Moore and his wife, Barbara. Alden is the founder and CEO of Moore Entertainment."

"Are you the one who ran the story about the Twin Rattlers' malfunction?" Alden asked.

The reporter nodded sheepishly.

"Well, Truvy, you may actually have done us a favor by running that article," Alden said. "Because that meant we had to give you something positive to write about next time. I know you'll do us proud. Won't you?"

"If everything is as fabulous on the inside as it was during the opening ceremony, I'm sure I will have many great things to say," Truvy said.

Brodie spoke into his walkie-talkie, calling for the media specialist he had assigned to accompany her around the park. "I have someone who will make sure you get the VIP treatment today."

The woman laughed and blushed and shook everyone's hand one more time before she disappeared into the park with her guide.

Putty in our hands.

Moments later, Alden and Barbara said their goodbyes—he would come back to the park on another day. In so many words, he admitted that the excitement of the opening ceremonies had pushed him to his limits—at least for today.

Now, armed with walkie-talkies, Brodie and Caitlyn stood face-to-face in the midst of the people milling about, gathering their families, getting their tickets and making plans of how to best see the park.

"Are you okay?" Brodie asked. He reached out to place a hand on her arm, but she flinched and pulled away.

"*Don't.* I'm fine." She raised her chin a notch, as if proving as much. "I will take my post at the back half of the park. You're going to cover the front half, right?"

The edge in her voice was chilly, but her words and demeanor were strictly professional. Two coworkers coming together for a common cause that had nothing to do with anything personal.

As she turned and walked away, regret prickled up Brodie's spine. He reminded himself that he couldn't have it both ways. He was here to do a job, not get tangled up in emotions. And his job he would complete at closing time. After that, an ocean would separate him from Caitlyn Moore.

A muffled voice sounded over the walkie-talkie, "Twenty-four? Come in, twenty-four."

That was his radio call number.

"This is Brodie."

"There are some people here looking for you at the west gate, Mr. Fortune Hayes. It's your family."

He gritted his teeth. He really didn't have time for them. He needed to get to his post inside the park. But he remembered how loving and patient Caitlyn had been with her parents, and he decided to borrow a page from her book. Just this once.

"Tell them I will be right there."

Brodie made his way through the people milling about and saw his mother, who had obviously spotted him first because she was waving them over. Next to her was his aunt Jeanne Marie, uncle Deke and his cousins, Stacey, Jude, Liam, Toby, Galen and Delaney, with her fiancé Cisco Mendoza. His brother Jensen was there, too, no doubt to see Amber perform. They'd left the babies with a sitter, but Toby's kids were very excited to be there.

Oh, and there's Orlando Mendoza standing next to Mum. Looking quite cozy, too. Hmm.

They greeted him enthusiastically. His cousins slapping him on the back and joking with him about how nice it was to have an inside source for free tickets.

"I hate to disappoint you," he said. "But that was a one-time perk."

His family laughed and slapped him on the back.

They think I'm joking.

"You know, the jury here is still out on how we feel about Cowboy Country USA," said Deke. "But we're your family, and we had to show up to support you and let you know how proud we are of you for the inroads you've made as you tried to make this theme park harmonious with our community. Offering the residents free admission was nothing short of genius, my boy. Not that I'm a businessman. But I know when a gesture feels genuine. You did good, son."

Suddenly, he felt like the Memorial Day Scrooge. Not only had his family turned up, but he was also starting to believe he had been too hasty when it came to writing off Caitlyn's idea. Maybe he had been a little too focused on winning and making the opening a success.

Even if he did need to keep emotions in check, perhaps an apology was in order. An acknowledgment that he was wrong, and Caitlyn was right.

Maybe he needed to loosen up just a little bit. The ribbon-cutting had gone off without a hitch. Nobody had been trampled in the crowd of people wanting to be the first guests to step foot into the park. And right now communication over the walkie-talkie indicated it was business as planned. There were no crises. Or at least none that needed his assistance.

You're going to be in the park, anyway. Why not give your family the VIP tour?

Brodie pulled a sheet of paper out of his back pocket— a schedule of the street shows that would be taking place and the various seated shows.

"Let's hurry up and get inside," he said. "The very first Main Street Shootout is about to take place. You won't want to miss it."

Brodie deftly directed them to a place outside the saloon where they would have the best view. They'd barely turned around when two classic cowboys—one wearing a white hat and the other wearing a black hat, both clad in jeans and plaid shirts with gun belts slung low on their hips, tumbled out of the saloon and started making a ruckus.

Guests stopped and stared wide-eyed at the two

actors as the cacophony they were creating acceler-
ated. The casting department had done a wonderful
job in choosing the actors. That was something that
had been in place long before he had arrived, and one
of the things that Moore Entertainment had handled
exceptionally well.

That thought was seconded by his family's reactions.
They gasped in all the right places; cheered for the cowboy in the white hat and booed the bad guy. After the
bad guy had gotten his comeuppance, they'd cheered
and clapped.

"That was exceptional," said Josephine. "Well done,
son. I wish Amelia were here to see this."

"Yes, where is my sister? I thought she was looking
forward to joining you today."

"She was, but the baby didn't sleep very well last
night. She said the whole family was up with the child.
She's not sure if Clementine is coming down with something, and she didn't want to take a chance of bringing
her out in a crowd. Besides, as lovely as this place is, it
really is no place for an infant."

His mother was right. Family and children changed
your life. You were no longer free to do whatever suited
you; you had to think of others before yourself. His
mind tried to focus on the struggles he and Caitlyn
had experienced as they'd worked toward today and
how each of them had compromised in certain areas.
The strangest feeling washed over him—he hoped she
hadn't felt personally compromised.

"What's next?" asked Jeanne Marie.

As they walked away, a street performer came up

to them and took a hold of Galen's hand. She was an older woman, a little crone-ish, but perfect for her role of Wild West fortune teller. Dressed like a gypsy with a bandanna around her head, a peasant blouse and skirt with jangly coin belts, she was obviously a brave one, approaching his family with her act.

Brodie was delighted she was doing exactly what he had instructed the performers to do. They were to always be in character when they were out among the guests, and they were to engage with as many people as possible. Both factors were key to Cowboy Country's ambience.

The fortune teller turned Galen's hand palm up and traced lines with her finger.

"You're a handsome young man," she said, fluttering eyes adorned with long, glittery false eyelashes. "Would you like me to tell your fortune? I have good news."

She made a show of batting her lashes; Brodie thought it was a little hokey, but he had to give her points for effort.

"Good news?" Galen said. "I'm always up for some good news. Knock yourself out."

"I hope you're single," the woman said.

"Of course I am. Plan to stay that way, too."

"Not for long," the fortune teller said. "You will meet a woman in white and be married within the month."

Galen laughed.

"That's a good one," he said. "Not gonna happen. There's no one in my life right now, and I'm not looking. You've got a better shot at marrying off my cousin

Brodie here than you do me. In fact, I'm surprised he hasn't already proposed. The dude is smitten."

Brodie knew he should set his cousin straight, but how did one explain *complicated*? Especially when he didn't understand it himself?

"Speaking of," said Josephine. "Where is Caitlyn?"

Caitlyn stood in the back of the Wild West Show, watching the guests file in for the inaugural show and reminding herself to breathe.

She hadn't been able to shake the bad feeling that had plagued her since yesterday's near disaster. Good grief, when had she become such a nervous Nelly?

When the stakes had become so high. That's when.

She'd resisted telling her father about her trepidations about opening too soon. And apparently that was a good thing, because her fears seemed to be unfounded. It was approaching eleven o'clock, and everything seemed to be going off without a hitch. They would close the doors on the first day at six o'clock, and so far, everything seemed to be fine.

Just as Brodie had assured her it would be.

The thought made her smirk a bit to herself.

She hoped he would be a gentleman when they reviewed how the day had unfolded.

Of course he would be. If there was one constant thing about Brodie, he always knew how to put the appropriate spin on things.

Except when he didn't, and in that case, he somehow managed to win you over to his side. Whether you wanted to be on his side or not.

And she did want them to be on the same side. In the worst way.

You don't always get what you want.

She was just about to go down to the ring to check on the horses and make sure Amber felt comfortable performing the show, when she looked up and saw Brodie and his family filing into the pavilion.

Her heart gave a little tug. She loved the Fortunes so much. They had embraced her and made her feel like such a part of the family—that big, boisterous family of her dreams. They were so engaging she found it hard to drag her eyes away from them. That's when Josephine caught her staring.

"Caitlyn!" Brodie's mother waved and motioned her over.

Caitlyn kept her eyes fixed on Josephine, but she felt Brodie's gaze locked on her. The intensity was palpable. In fact, it was white-hot.

Dammit. She should have gone down to the ring when she'd had the chance. Now, if she didn't go over and greet them, it would look bad. Really bad.

Just because things hadn't worked out between her and Brodie didn't mean she couldn't remain friends with the Fortunes. She genuinely cared for these people, and she certainly didn't want to slight them today by ignoring them. After all, Caitlyn would be in Horseback Hollow as long as it took for her father to recover.

She summoned her courage and went over to say hello.

"There you are," Jeanne Marie said. "We were just talking about you. We came to the unanimous conclusion that we weren't leaving the park without seeing you."

"Wait, I wasn't involved in that *unanimous* decision." Galen winked at Caitlyn.

"That's because your vote doesn't count." Delaney elbowed her brother. "Besides, if we're going to find you a bride within the month, you're going to have to learn to be nice."

"He is nice," Caitlyn said. "Because of him, I know what it feels like to have a big brother."

"Actually, after you marry Brodie, we'll be cousins."

Caitlyn felt color bloom in her cheeks. She still couldn't bring herself to look at Brodie.

She cleared her throat. "So what is this about finding you a bride within the month?"

"The Wild West fortune teller picked Galen out of the crowd and delivered the message that he would marry a woman wearing white within the month."

The family poked fun at him, and the apparent love filled Caitlyn's heart to overflowing.

"Be sure to invite me to the wedding," Caitlyn said.

"Only if you invite me to yours." Galen cast a glance at Brodie, who was staring at his smartphone a little too intently. "Or if you're going to let a good thing get away, maybe I'll marry Caitlyn. Her blouse is white."

The comment made Brodie look up. His brows were knit together, and his expression suggested that he didn't find humor in Galen's joke.

Why not?

It was just a joke.

Then Brodie's expression neutralized. "We should find our seats."

"Please join us, Caitlyn," said Josephine.

"Oh, well, thank you, but no. I need to go make sure everything is okay for the performance."

"That's what your radio is for." It was the first time Brodie had spoken directly to her since this morning. "They have a stage manager and director. If they need you they can call you on your radio. Join us—please."

A spark of emotion flickered across his face.

Was this a peace offering?

Looking into those blue eyes she couldn't even remember why she was upset with him. Well, she could remember, but suddenly with all those Fortune faces staring at her, eagerly awaiting her answer, suddenly it didn't really matter anymore. Then when the music cued and the actors rode the horses into the ring, Caitlyn didn't have much of a choice.

As they took their seats, she noticed that Brodie stepped between her and Galen, causing his cousin to shift down a seat, putting Brodie right next to her.

Jeanne Marie was on Brodie's left. She leaned across and said, "We're having another barbecue before Brodie goes back to London. You make sure he brings you to the party."

That's right. He would be leaving after the park was successfully opened. She supposed she had been too preoccupied with work to remember that. Still, it didn't stop the dull ache in her heart that began to throb with Jeanne Marie's reminder.

Caitlyn was glad when the others began cheering

for Amber, who had majestically ridden into the ring. With her long, tousled blond hair and athletic build, she looked gorgeous on that horse. Caitlyn focused on how Amber really was the perfect person for the show.

She could see why the Moore Entertainment casting and advertising departments had wanted her to be the face of Cowboy Country USA, but she'd declined the opportunity, wanting to stick to the serious riding.

And that may not have been a bad way to go. Her spirited personality and expert riding skills shone brightly in the ring. A less-skilled rider probably couldn't have handled the horse. Caitlyn had all the confidence in the world in Amber, but she was still nervous for her.

And sad that Brodie would be leaving. He hadn't even told her when. Had he planned to?

As Amber put the horse through the routine, Caitlyn leaned forward in her seat. When she did, her knee bumped Brodie's. Subtly, she shifted her body to allow some space for those long, muscular legs.

Strong legs that made her a little weak in the knees.

Really, Caitlyn?

She refocused on Amber, who had just performed a rather awe-inspiring move with her horse, dancing it slalom-style through the dozen or so horses performing with her in the ring.

But a moment later, Brodie's knee was back against hers.

She had to fight the urge to nudge him away.

Actually, no, she didn't. A traitorous, idiotic part of her longed to reach out and touch his knee.

Instead, she slanted him a glance, hoping she looked a little disgusted. He gave her a single arched brow, which made her simultaneously thrilled and regretful of the flirtation.

Was this his way of trying to make up?

Damn him.

Damn him right to her bed.

No. Because he was leaving, and her heart was breaking all over again.

She needed to be stronger than to let a little knee bump—physical contact that wasn't really physical contact—lead her back into temptation. In addition to him leaving—abandoning her—he'd acted like such a jerk the past couple of weeks.

She had this strange thought that maybe he'd been trying to distance himself because he knew he was leaving. That the closer they became, the harder it would be to leave. She wanted to tell him that was just ridiculous. Pushing her away wasn't going to work.

She leaned toward him to ask if they could talk later. This alternating silence and arguing was just ridiculous. They were both better than that. They'd proved that by working together and getting to where they were today. But before she could form the words, a cap gun misfired in the ring. Amber's horse reared back on its hind legs. The misstep must've surprised Amber because she lost her grip and fell backward. She landed in front of another show horse, and that scared him, sending him into rearing panic mode.

One of the cowboy actors managed to jump off his horse and scoop up Amber. If he'd been a second longer she would've been trampled. But in doing so he'd had to let go of his horse, and that's when all hell broke loose.

The other horses got spooked, causing them to throw their riders. One of the horses knocked over one of the barrels and some other props in the ring. The noises mixed with the screams and shouting from the audience as guests knocked each other down to run out of the pavilion.

Caitlyn, Brodie and his family sprang to life, jumping over overturned chairs and dodging people, as they tried to make their way to the front of the ring. But they were too late. By the time they'd gotten down front, at least nine horses had broken loose and stampeded out of the ring, running rampant through the park.

"Here, grab some rope," shouted Deke. He tossed some that was used for props to the men. "Let's get out there before those animals manage to kill someone."

Chapter Thirteen

A number of men—a combination of park employees, locals and Fortunes—had managed to wrangle and subdue all nine of the horses before they could hurt anyone else. While the damage to the park and the Wild West Show area was major, the actors' injuries were minor and none of the park guests were hurt.

Still, that didn't even begin to cover the real damage that had been done.

People had captured the mayhem on video cameras and smartphones, and now Cowboy Country's stampeding horses were all over the evening news—and not just locally. The story had hit the wire services and internet and accounts of "Horsegate USA" had gone viral.

Members of the media who had been invited to the grand opening had managed to pick out the mouthiest, most colorful people to interview, and they had lambasted Moore Entertainment for endangering everyone's welfare.

The animal handlers and the Fortunes had secured the horses, and the managerial staff had cleared the park and closed the gates by one o'clock. The minute Caitlyn had gotten back to the executive offices, she was greeted with a stack of nearly one hundred phone messages that Janie had taken from additional media asking for interviews.

Brodie had instructed all of the department heads to round up their staff members and bring them to the all-purpose room in the training facility. He would give each employee strict instructions not to talk to the media. He was the only person who was allowed to say anything about Cowboy Country USA in any capacity to the press.

As far as Caitlyn was concerned, he could shoulder that responsibility on his own.

She took the stack of messages from Janie and deposited them on Brodie's neat desk, barely able to contain the slow simmer of resentment.

They hadn't been ready to open the park.

Caitlyn knew that, too well. She'd tried to warn Brodie, but he'd used his veto power over common sense to rush the opening.

Safety be damned, all in the name of getting in and getting the park opened and impressing her father.

There you go, mastermind. Get us out of this mess.

When she got to her office, Janie was buzzing her.

"If it's someone from the media, please take a message. Mr. Fortune Hayes will be handling all media contact."

"No, I'm sorry, Ms. Moore. Your father is on line one. He said it's urgent."

Crap.

In the midst of everything she tried to call him once, but hadn't had time to call back. As eager as Brodie was to please him, now she thought her father would've been the first person Brodie had contacted. Obviously not.

Oh, wait, Brodie Fortune Hayes only dealt in miracles and glory.

She just hoped this episode hadn't set her father back. He'd been so happy this morning at the ribbon-cutting. How had things spiraled out of control so fast?

She let out a carefully controlled breath, and picked up the phone. "Hi, Dad. Please don't worry. We have everything under control."

She spit the words out in one breath because she knew if she didn't, she wouldn't be able to get a word in edgewise.

"Are you kidding me? Are you *kidding* me? How can you say you have everything under control when we are the laughingstock of the evening news? The international news. I can't believe this. Hayes isn't picking up his phone—"

"He is debriefing the employees right now. He's instructing them not to talk to the media. I'm sorry you're upset. I tried to call you, but I didn't want to leave a message on voice mail."

She'd tried to call him, but he hadn't picked up. Caitlyn figured he was either resting or maybe if he got a second wind on the trip back to Lubbock, he and her mother had stopped to get something to eat.

"It was an emergency. Then we had to take care of business, Dad. Brodie is still debriefing the staff, and I just got back into the office."

"Don't take that tone with me. I should've been the *first* one you called. Instead, I had to hear this on the news."

He was yelling now. Full-out yelling. Caitlyn had to hold the phone away from her ear.

"Dad, you were the first one I called. I couldn't get in touch with you. I was in the midst of an emergency I didn't have time to keep dialing you. Calm down—"

"Don't you dare tell me to calm down. I trusted you, Caitlyn. I put my faith in you, and you let me down. I can't remember a time when I've ever been this disappointed in you."

"Dad—"

"Actually, no. You know what? You let yourself down. This disaster was caused by animals, Caitlyn. *Animals*. You are a zoologist. Animals are your area of expertise. If anyone could have prevented this from happening, it was you. You failed. Now I know. It just doesn't make good business sense for me to invest in this zoo park dream of yours. You might as well pack your bags and go back to your research in Chicago."

Caitlyn was too stunned to respond. Just as well, because after he had said his piece, he hung up.

She sat in her chair staring out the window, holding the receiver, and thinking about calling him back.

But why?

So she could absolve herself of the blame? Tell him

that it was his own blindness and Brodie's pigheaded-
ness that created the disaster?

No. Because she knew she was just as much to blame.
She'd gone against her instincts when she'd known the
animals weren't settled and comfortable enough with
their surroundings and there were props in use.

She'd let Brodie steamroll her. And that was nobody's fault but her own.

From here on out, she resolved, she would not allow
herself to be crushed. By anyone.

Telling on Brodie wasn't going to fix anything. The
damage had already been done.

She turned around to hang up the telephone receiver
and saw Brodie standing in her office doorway.

"Was that your father?"

Caitlyn nodded. It felt as if she didn't have any words
left. But really, what was she supposed to say?

"I was going to call him after I finished the media
counseling. How was he?"

She glared at him. "How do you suppose he was?
Did you send everyone home?"

"Everyone except security and the stable managers
and staff. They're working with the vet to make sure
the animals are okay. I sent the others home with the
promise of a full day's pay."

Playing the hero again.

Caitlyn gave herself a mental shake. Being catty
wasn't going to solve anything. It certainly wasn't making her feel better.

"It sounds like you have everything under control.
So I'm going to leave."

"Where? Wait—what?" He waved away his words. "It's been a stressful day. I totally understand if you need to get away for a bit. Take the rest of the afternoon. Do what you need to do. I'll see you tomorrow."

She shook her head.

"No, Brodie. I don't think you understand. I'm leaving. I'm going back to Chicago. You don't need me. You can handle everything just fine on your own."

Brodie shook his head. "Caitlyn, I understand what it's like to live with a father you can't please."

She looked up at his non sequitur.

"Nice try, Brodie. But I don't think you fully get it. Sir Simon may have shipped you off to boarding school, but it sounds like he gave you a pretty good life. Look at you. You're confident. You're successful. You're a world-class business consultant. If life at boarding school hurt you, it didn't leave any noticeable scars."

She knew that wasn't altogether true. This man was so emotionally unavailable that something had happened to make him that way, something beyond the woman who broke his heart. But she didn't want to think about that right now, because she was saying goodbye. Someone else could try to save Brodie Fortune Hayes.

She was done.

He stepped inside her office and closed the door.

"When I was thirteen years old, I decided I wanted to go see my birth father. His name was Rhys Henry Hayes. He and my mother divorced when I was three. So I really didn't remember him. Oliver couldn't stand him. He used to just rage on about what a bastard the guy was, but I didn't believe him. You see, Oliver was super protective of our mother. He was seven when our dad left. I always thought his attitude toward our dad was colored by childhood resentment.

"I couldn't take his word for it. I had to find out for myself. So it was Christmas. Just before we were to return home for the holiday, I ran away from that fancy boarding school that you were ribbing me about a moment ago. I bummed a ride from a classmate and made my way to London. I was determined to find my father. He was living in a flat in Chelsea and I thought he was going to be the coolest guy in the world. He was going to put that stuffed shirt of a stepfather of mine to shame. He was my dad. He was my superhero. Or at least that's how I'd built him up in my naive little-boy mind. When he answered the door, he looked at me like I was garbage. He asked me what the bloody hell I was doing there and how dare I show up unannounced.

"Long story short, he told me he wanted nothing to do with me. I was nothing but an inconvenience to him. When I showed my disappointment, he told me I was weak, and my reaction to his words proved I would never amount to anything. He said, 'Your brother Oliver is ten times the man you will ever be and I want nothing to do with him. What makes you think I'd welcome you into my life?' I opened myself up, rendered myself vulnerable to the one person in this world I thought would show me unconditional love, and he spit in my face. Figuratively, of course. But it would have hurt a lot less if he had actually done it."

They were both quiet for a moment. Caitlyn was trying her hardest not to let his heartrending story of rejection break down her armor.

"Just so you understand why I'm telling you the story," he said. "It's not to prove that one of our dads was worse than the other or that one of our struggles was less than the other. Each person's struggle makes them who they are, and in some ways—in many ways— it defines them. I know my experience with my natural father has defined me. But in many ways you have changed me. You have helped me see that it's okay to let people in. That not everybody has bad intentions. I'm sorry if you think that of me. I hope you don't."

After Brodie left her office, Caitlyn sat there thinking for a long time.

Her workaholic father had always been hard and blustery, but she'd never had any doubt that she was his princess.

A princess he'd set on a shelf, out of harm's way— giving her a job instead of making her find a job; indulging her with lip service about her dream of opening a zoo park; patronizing her by letting her take over his office while he was sick, but never really believing that she could make a difference.

But the truth was she'd never doubted his love. The comparison of Brodie's verbally abusive father to her own—well, there was no comparison. She was the one who had been soft all these years. She was the one who had allowed people to walk on her.

That's why she needed to leave and start taking responsibility for herself.

* * *

Brodie had to fix this disaster. He would fix it. Even if it meant driving to Lubbock to talk to Alden Moore face-to-face, which was exactly what he was doing. Everything at the park was secured. They would be closed tomorrow, of course, as they started putting the pieces back together.

In the meantime, he was going to talk to Alden Moore. It seemed like the best way to get on the road to making things right.

This went beyond business and reputations and referrals for Japanese theme parks. His stubbornness had nearly broken *them*. It all became crystal clear as he watched Caitlyn walk away.

Now her words still rang in his ears: *You don't need me. You can handle everything just fine on your own.*

She was wrong.

He did need her.

He'd needed her since the moment he'd first set eyes on her in February. It was rather perverse how it took almost losing someone to snap everything into place. Now he knew that he'd been afraid, he'd been too long on his own, yet the thought of loving and losing again terrified him.

Funny thing, he thought he was trying to protect his heart, and all the while he was setting it up to be broken into tiny pieces. As he drove, he knew that even if it took an entire village to prove how much he needed her, he'd make this right.

He was going to win her back.

His phone rang, and he activated the hands-free device.

"Hello?"

"Brodie? It's your mum. Jeanne Marie, uncle Deke and I are worried about you, love. We want to know how you're doing. Is everything all right?"

It felt odd asking for help. Uncomfortable. Unnatural. When you asked for help, opened yourself up wide, you rendered yourself vulnerable. Ever since his encounter with Rhys Henry Hayes, Brodie had done his damnedest to button himself up and not let people in. That's why he'd become the spin master. When he painted happy pictures for the world, no one was ever the wiser of the thirteen-year-old boy who was still crying inside.

Funny, wasn't it, how he thought he was going to help Caitlyn Moore, but it was she who had made him over from the inside?

"Actually, if I may be honest, I've just about hit rock bottom. But I know what I need to do to fix this. But I'll need the help of my family to make things better."

Chapter Fourteen

Caitlyn had been in such a state yesterday that she'd gone off and left her wallet at the office. She hadn't realized it right away, of course. It was only when she had gone to book her airline ticket back to Chicago that she missed it.

By that time it was late, and she didn't want to drive from Vicker's Corners all the way back to Horseback Hollow to get it. Especially when she wasn't even certain that was where she had left it.

Plus, she didn't want to take a chance of running into Brodie, who most likely would still be at the office even at that hour. She was exhausted and much too vulnerable to risk running into him.

Early the next morning, she'd called Janie and asked

her to check for the wallet. Sure enough, it had fallen out in her desk drawer, the place where she kept her purse.

Hearing Janie's voice made her realize that would've been cowardly to leave without saying goodbye in person. She would've called, of course. She wouldn't have just disappeared without telling Janie where she was going.

But it was much better to do this in person.

More difficult, but better.

She was all packed and ready to go, suitcases in the car. The plan was to grab her wallet, say her goodbyes then hightail it to the airport where she would buy her ticket and board the plane. She would be back in Chicago by late afternoon.

She wasn't the least bit excited about the trip, but it was better than hanging around a place where she was superfluous. Who knew if she would even stay in Chicago? But she would regroup there and figure out what she wanted to do next.

What she wanted to do with the rest of her life.

The thought took her breath away, not in an entirely good way. She needed to stop being afraid of the unknown.

She just hoped she didn't run into Brodie this morning.

He would probably already be out in the park, supervising the cleanup. She hoped she'd miss him this morning.

No, she didn't.

Good grief, Caitlyn. After everything? Don't be an idiot.

She parked in her usual spot, got out of the car like

she had every morning since she'd come to work at Cowboy Country and started to make her way toward the executive offices, but she stopped when she saw a caravan of vehicles pulling into the employee parking lot. There must've been twenty-five or thirty of them—gosh, maybe even thirty-five? She wouldn't have given it much thought, but then people she recognized started piling out—every single one of them was a Fortune or Mendoza or somebody else from Horseback Hollow that she recognized from the wedding or the barbecue or the town council meeting. There was a whole parade of them, arriving with ladders and toolboxes. They all wore blue jeans; some wore plaid shirts, others sported T-shirts and most of them sported cowboy hats.

Caitlyn spied Deke and Galen. They waved at her.

"Good morning, sunshine," said Galen. "I'll bet today's going to be a much better day than yesterday. I see you wore your work clothes." He lifted a questioning brow as he took in her dress and heels. "Here, help Tim Marcus carry in this coil of rope, will you? By the way, Caitlyn, this is Tim. Tim, this is Caitlyn. She's my cousin Brodie's girl."

Caitlyn nearly choked.

Galen winked at her, and his harmless teasing made her heart squeeze. She couldn't bring herself to dispute him and explain that no, in fact she was not Brodie's girl. Never had been. Never would be.

So she changed the subject. "What are you doing? Why are you all here this morning? The park is closed."

Galen cocked his head in mock exasperation. "Well,

obviously we're not here to play. I don't usually bring my toolbox to a day at the amusement park."

"We're here to help clean up the park, to get you guys back up and running again," Deke offered as he walked by, carrying a power saw. "Didn't Brodie tell you? He asked us to come."

"Really? All of you?"

Everyone in Horseback Hollow hated Cowboy Country USA. Why in the world would they do this? Why would they help them?

"Deke, no, Brodie didn't tell me."

"Well, you'll have to take that up with him. I need to get this inside. This is heavy. There's a couple gallons of paint in the bed of my truck. Why don't you toss that rope over your shoulder and grab the paint? We've got a lot of work to do, and we aren't getting anything done by standing around talking."

Caitlyn was speechless. This just didn't add up. She thought these people were ready to run them out of town on a rail. Why would they give their time to help out the place that had essentially been put out of commission?

Then it hit her.

Of course. It was so obvious.

What Cowboy Country had been missing, that something that she just couldn't seem to put her finger on was the influence of *real cowboys*.

Well, here they were today, as if heaven sent.

She put the rope over her shoulder and grabbed the paint buckets. She caught up with Deke just inside the gates. He was talking to Brodie.

Brodie did a double take, and his face brightened.

"Good morning. I'm glad you're here. Even if it does spoil the surprise I had planned for you."

Surprise?

What was he talking about?

"Did you hire all these people to put the park back together?" she asked.

"Heck, no," Deke interjected. "This is what real cowboys are about. Helping each other out in times of trouble. We always put personal differences aside when people are in need. If you'll excuse me, I'm going to get to work. Are you here to work or talk?"

Exactly. Real cowboys.

She couldn't very well walk out now. Not when all of these good people had shown up out of the goodness of their own hearts to help out.

She turned back to Brodie. "Did you round up all these people?"

A grin spread over his face. "I did. I realized since it was my fault for not listening to you that I had better fix everything, and fast. You won't find anyone more reliable than these folks. With everyone pitching in, we can have this place good as new and ready to open by the end of the week."

"Excuse me? Did I hear you right? Did you just admit that you should've listened to me?"

"You're absolutely right. I should've listened."

Was this the first time she was seeing the real Brodie? Because there seemed to be no spin on this. No pretense or sleight-of-hand. This just might be the real deal. The real man.

But she couldn't quite let herself believe.

"Brodie, you're so good at what you do, but sometimes you won't get out of your own way."

"I can't argue that point with you," he said. "Sometimes I am my own worst enemy. But today I want you to know how deeply sorry I am and I want to show you that I can make things right."

"Since you're the man with the plan," she said, "tell me where you want me to jump in."

Brodie eyed her dress. "You can't work out here dressed like that. Don't worry about it. We have plenty of people."

"This is your lucky day. I just happen to have some casual clothes in my car. Let me change and I'll be all yours."

Brodie's eyes softened, and for a moment she saw so much emotion in those incredible blue eyes that her heart nearly overflowed. She wanted to hug him or at least touch him, but she couldn't. She might not make the flight to Chicago that was leaving this morning, but there was another one this evening. She would be on that one.

So she smiled at him, a sad smile full of regret, full of everything she had hoped that they could be, but would never be and she turned to get her clothes.

"Caitlyn?"

She turned back toward him.

"I'm sorry. For everything. I wish we could try—"

Oh, no. She was slipping. She could feel the steel pin of her heart being pulled toward the magnet of his soul.

Then felt him pull away and saw his wall go back up. *What is wrong with him?*

"Caitlyn." It was her father's voice. She turned around, and there he was. There was Alden Moore with a hammer in his hand. "Good morning, to both of you."

"Dad? What are you doing here?"

"Well, I'm here to work."

"What do you mean?" She looked to Brodie. "Did you tell him what you were doing today?"

"I did."

"But Dad, I think it's too soon for you to be doing manual labor."

Come to think of it, she couldn't recall a time that she'd ever seen her father doing manual labor. He'd always hired somebody to do the job that needed tending.

"You're probably right. But I've also come to talk to you."

He slanted a glance at Brodie and smiled.

What's going on?

"Someone drove to Lubbock yesterday and paid me a visit. During which I learned that you are actually the brains and the heart behind this operation. And I believe I owe you an apology."

Caitlyn shot an astonished glance at Brodie.

He shrugged.

"Brodie told me you tried to convince him that the park wasn't ready to open. We should've listened to you. I promise I will start doing just that right now. And I'm sorry for doubting you. So that's all. Since the doctor says it's too soon for physical labor, how about if I take this opportunity to walk the park and get a feel for the lay of the land? I need to figure out where that zoo park would be best situated. I'll leave you two alone, because I think you have some things to discuss."

As her father walked away, Caitlyn turned to Brodie.

"You did that? You went and talked to my dad yesterday? And he organized the work crew today?"

Brodie smiled at her, and there were those dimples that melted her heart.

"Guilty as charged. But only on the first count. For the work crew, I simply asked my family if they could pitch in. It seems that if you ask for a couple of Fortunes, you end up with the entire town. That should say something about the going rate of a Fortune these days."

And there was that sense of humor that she couldn't resist.

"I'm overwhelmed," she said. "I don't know what to say except for thank you. Thank you for setting things right with my father. Thank you for bringing all these people here today to help—"

Brodie put a finger up to Caitlyn's lips. "I'm the one who should be thanking you. As I quite ineloquently tried to say yesterday afternoon, since I met you, I have seen you put your heart and soul on the line for the people and things that you love and believe in. You've taken risks and exposed yourself, and through it all you always remain true to yourself. You have taught me how strong vulnerability can make a person. I said yesterday there was one person in the world who had made an impression on me so strong that it changed me—and not in a good way. But I am so fortunate to have met someone who has made a similar lasting impression on me and has changed me for the better. That person is you, Caitlyn Moore."

He reached out and took her hand, tentatively at first. She laced her fingers through his to show him it was okay. "I wanted you to know that I'm ready to have a relationship, to open my heart and be part of something greater than myself." Then he pulled her into his arms and lowered his lips to hers. He kissed her long and slow, and she had no doubt that she was going to miss that flight to Chicago tonight.

He pulled away and cupped her face in his hands. "I love you, Caitlyn."

"I love you, too. Don't you ever let anyone tell you you don't have a heart."

"I don't," he said. "Because now it belongs to you."

* * * * *

*Don't miss the next installment of the new
Harlequin Special Edition continuity*
**THE FORTUNES OF TEXAS:
COWBOY COUNTRY**

*Cowboy Galen Fortune Jones thinks he's not
cut out for marriage, until he agrees to be
Aurora McElroy's pretend husband for a week.
But once they start playing house, he discovers
some very real feelings for his make-believe bride...*

*Look for
FORTUNE'S JUNE BRIDE*
by New York Times *Bestselling Author Allison Leigh
On sale June 2015, wherever Harlequin books
and ebooks are sold.*

COMING NEXT MONTH FROM

H HARLEQUIN®

SPECIAL EDITION

Available May 19, 2015

#2407 FORTUNE'S JUNE BRIDE
The Fortunes of Texas: Cowboy Country • by Allison Leigh
Galen Fortune Jones isn't the marrying kind...until he's roped into playing groom at the new Cowboy Country theme park in Horseback Hollow, Texas. His "bride," beautiful Aurora McElroy, piques his interest, especially when she needs a real-life fake husband. This one cowboy may have just met his match!

#2408 THE PRINCESS AND THE SINGLE DAD
Royal Babies • by Leanne Banks
Princess Sasha of Sergenia fled her dangerous home country for the principality of Chantaine. There, she assumes another identity: nanny to handsome construction specialist Gavin Sinclair's two adorable children. As the princess falls hard for the proud papa, can she form a royal family of her very own?

#2409 HER RED-CARPET ROMANCE
Matchmaking Mamas • by Marie Ferrarella
Film producer Lukas Spader needs to get his work life in order, so he hires professional organizer Yohanna Andrzejewski. She's temptingly beautiful, but Lukas must keep his eyes on his job, not his stunning new employee. As Cupid's arrow strikes them both, though, Yohanna might just fix her sexy boss's life into a happily-ever-after!

#2410 THE INSTANT FAMILY MAN
The Barlow Brothers • by Shirley Jump
Luke Barlow is happily living the single life in Stone Gap, North Carolina—until his ex's gorgeous little sister, Peyton Reynolds, shows up. She announces Luke is now the caretaker for a four-year-old daughter he never knew about. Determined to be a good dad, Luke tries to create a home for little Maddy and her aunt, one that might just be for forever...

#2411 DYLAN'S DADDY DILEMMA
The Colorado Fosters • by Tracy Madison
Chelsea Bell needs help—fast. The single mom has landed in Steamboat Springs, Colorado, and is out of money. So when dashing Dylan Foster offers her and her son, Henry, a place to stay, Chelsea's floored. Why would a complete stranger offer her help, let alone bond with her little boy? This is just the first surprise in store for one unexpected family.

#2412 FALLING FOR THE MOM-TO-BE
Home in Heartlandia • by Lynne Marshall
Ever since his wife passed away, Leif Andersen has had no time for love. Enter Marta Hoyas, a beautiful—and *pregnant!*—artist who's in town to paint a local mural. She's also living in Leif's house while she does so. The last thing Marta wants is to fall for someone who couldn't be a father to her unborn child, but Leif might just be the perfect dad-to-be.

YOU CAN FIND MORE INFORMATION ON UPCOMING HARLEQUIN® TITLES, FREE EXCERPTS AND MORE AT WWW.HARLEQUIN.COM.

HSECNM0515

REQUEST YOUR FREE BOOKS!
2 FREE NOVELS PLUS 2 FREE GIFTS!

⊞ HARLEQUIN®

SPECIAL EDITION
Life, Love & Family

YES! Please send me 2 FREE Harlequin® Special Edition novels and my 2 FREE gifts (gifts are worth about $10). After receiving them, if I don't wish to receive any more books, I can return the shipping statement marked "cancel." If I don't cancel, I will receive 6 brand-new novels every month and be billed just $4.74 per book in the U.S. or $5.49 per book in Canada. That's a savings of at least 12% off the cover price! It's quite a bargain! Shipping and handling is just 50¢ per book in the U.S. and 75¢ per book in Canada.* I understand that accepting the 2 free books and gifts places me under no obligation to buy anything. I can always return a shipment and cancel at any time. Even if I never buy another book, the two free books and gifts are mine to keep forever.

235/335 HDN GH3Z

Name _____ (PLEASE PRINT) _____

Address _____ Apt. # _____

City _____ State/Prov. _____ Zip/Postal Code _____

Signature (if under 18, a parent or guardian must sign)

Mail to the **Reader Service:**
IN U.S.A.: P.O. Box 1867, Buffalo, NY 14240-1867
IN CANADA: P.O. Box 609, Fort Erie, Ontario L2A 5X3

Want to try two free books from another line?
Call 1-800-873-8635 or visit www.ReaderService.com.

* Terms and prices subject to change without notice. Prices do not include applicable taxes. Sales tax applicable in N.Y. Canadian residents will be charged applicable taxes. Offer not valid in Quebec. This offer is limited to one order per household. Not valid for current subscribers to Harlequin Special Edition books. All orders subject to credit approval. Credit or debit balances in a customer's account(s) may be offset by any other outstanding balance owed by or to the customer. Please allow 4 to 6 weeks for delivery. Offer available while quantities last.

Your Privacy—The Reader Service is committed to protecting your privacy. Our Privacy Policy is available online at www.ReaderService.com or upon request from the Reader Service.

We make a portion of our mailing list available to reputable third parties that offer products we believe may interest you. If you prefer that we not exchange your name with third parties, or if you wish to clarify or modify your communication preferences, please visit us at www.ReaderService.com/consumerschoice or write to us at Reader Service Preference Service, P.O. Box 9062, Buffalo, NY 14240-9062. Include your complete name and address.

HSE15

Galen tucked the "deed" into his shirt and nudged along
his horse, Blaze, with a squeeze of his knees. He set his
white hat more firmly on his head so it wouldn't go blow-
ing off when they made their mad dash down Main. "But
I'm definitely not looking for a career change. Ranching's
in my blood. Only thing I ever wanted to do. Amusing as
this might be for now, I'll be happy as hell to hand over
Rusty's hat to whoever they get to replace Joey." He took
in the other riders as well as Cabot and gathered his reins.
"Y'all ready?"

They nodded, and as one, they set off in a thunder of
horse hooves.

Eleven minutes later on the dot, he was pulling Aurora
into his arms after "knocking" Frank off his feet, saying "I do" to Harlan's Preacher Man and bending Aurora
low over his arm while the audience—always larger on a

Saturday—clapped and hooted.

Unfortunately for Galen, the longer he'd gone without Rusty actually kissing Lila, the more he couldn't stop thinking about it as he pressed his cheek against Aurora's, her head tucked down in his chest.

"Big crowd," he whispered. The mikes were dead and he held her a little longer than usual. Because of the lengthy applause they were getting, of course.

"Too big," she whispered back. "You going to let me up anytime soon?"

He immediately straightened, and she smiled broadly at the crowd, waving her hand as she tucked her hand through his arm and they strolled offstage.

But he could see through the smile to the frustration brewing in her blue eyes.

He waited until they were well away from the stage. "Sorry about that."

"About what?" She impatiently pushed her veil behind her back and kept looking over her shoulder as they strode through the side street. She was damn near jogging, and the beads hanging from her dress were bouncing.

"Holding the…uh…the…uh…" He yanked his string tie loose, feeling like an idiot. "You know. The embrace."

She gave him a distracted look. "What about it?"

"Holding it so long."

Don't miss
FORTUNE'S JUNE BRIDE
by Allison Leigh,
available June 2015 wherever
Harlequin® Special Edition books and ebooks are sold.

www.Harlequin.com